MONTANA MAVERICKS

Welcome to Big Sky Country, home of the Montana Mavericks! Where free-spirited men and women discover love on the range.

THE TRAIL TO TENACITY

Tenacity is the town that time forgot, home of down-to-earth cowboys who'd give you the (denim) shirt off their back. Through the toughest times, they've held their heads high, and they've never lost hope. Take a ride out this way and get to know the neighbors—you might even meet the maverick of your dreams!

Win Jackson is a dream in the form of a cowboy, and second-grade schoolteacher Stacy Abernathy falls for him fast. The widowed rancher has made it clear he doesn't do serious. But Stacy can't help herself; the single dad and his boys are clearly in need of some TLC, and she is the perfect person to deliver it—even if she risks breaking her own heart in the process.

Dear Reader,

Fall is coming to Bronco, Montana. Leaves are beginning to turn red and gold, fireplaces are crackling and, even better, school is starting. And that makes Stacy Abernathy declare fall her favorite time of the year. As a teacher at Bronco Elementary School, she's eager to get back into the classroom after the long summer break. Dealing with her little students doesn't give her time to dwell on the fact that she's still single with not even one steady boyfriend to call her own.

Widower Win Jackson has moved himself and his two sons, Joshua and Oliver, to Bronco to start a new life. With his sons to raise, a ranch to build and his job as the new agribusiness teacher at Bronco High School, Win is a busy man. He doesn't need or want a relationship. And he certainly doesn't need his talkative young son trying to hook him up with a pretty blonde teacher. But after Win takes one look at Stacy, he can't forget her. And soon he begins to wonder if a man can truly love again.

It's always such fun for me to visit the world of the Montana Mavericks, and I hope you enjoy strolling the streets of Bronco again and reading how two lonely teachers finally realize that together they make the perfect family.

Stella Bagwell

THE MAVERICK
MAKES THE GRADE

STELLA BAGWELL

Harlequin

MONTANA MAVERICKS

Special thanks and acknowledgment are given to
Stella Bagwell for her contribution to the
Montana Mavericks: The Trail to Tenacity miniseries.

Harlequin®
MONTANA MAVERICKS

Recycling programs
for this product may
not exist in your area.

ISBN-13: 978-1-335-14313-6

The Maverick Makes the Grade

Copyright © 2024 by Harlequin Enterprises ULC

For questions and comments about the quality of this book, please contact us at CustomerService@Harlequin.com.

Harlequin Enterprises ULC
22 Adelaide St. West, 41st Floor
Toronto, Ontario M5H 4E3, Canada
www.Harlequin.com

Printed in Lithuania

MIX
Paper | Supporting
responsible forestry
FSC® C021394

After writing more than one hundred books for Harlequin, **Stella Bagwell** still finds writing about two people discovering everlasting love very rewarding. She loves all things Western and has been married to her own real cowboy for fifty-one years. Living on the south Texas coast, she also enjoys being outdoors and helping her husband care for the animals on the small ranch they call home. The couple has one son, who teaches high school mathematics and coaches football and powerlifting.

Books by Stella Bagwell

Montana Mavericks: The Trail to Tenacity

The Maverick Makes the Grade

Harlequin Special Edition

Men of the West

Her Kind of Doctor
The Arizona Lawman
Her Man on Three Rivers Ranch
A Ranger for Christmas
His Texas Runaway
Home to Blue Stallion Ranch
The Rancher's Best Gift
Her Man Behind the Badge
His Forever Texas Rose
The Baby That Binds Them
Sleigh Ride with the Rancher
The Wrangler Rides Again
The Other Hollister Man
Rancher to the Rescue
The Cowboy's Road Trip

Visit the Author Profile page
at Harlequin.com for more titles.

To all the wonderful teachers who dedicate their lives
to helping young students be the best they can be.

Chapter One

Stacy Abernathy was pinning red and gold paper leaves to the edge of a bulletin board when a movement beyond the open door of her classroom caught the corner of her eye. The last bell of the school day had rung a while ago and the students had already exited the Bronco Elementary School building, so when she looked over her shoulder for a closer look, she expected to see a janitor or a fellow teacher. Instead, she spotted a fairly tall boy with a shock of dark blond hair and an olive-green pack resting against his back. He was clearly too old for her second-grade class, which would make him a student in Dante Sanchez's third-grade group or Reginald Porter's fourth-grade class.

Placing the remaining decorations aside, Stacy walked over to where the boy continued to stand just beyond the doorway.

"Hi!" he greeted her. "Are you a teacher?"

"I'm Ms. Abernathy," she informed him. "What's your name?"

"I'm Oliver Jackson," he said with a grin. "I'm in fourth grade. Mr. Porter is my teacher."

He was a cute kid, Stacy thought, with long, lanky limbs and bangs that fell over one eye. A spattering of freckles dotted the bridge of his nose while dimples dented both rounded cheeks. Because the school wasn't all that large, she usually recognized all the students and could call them by name. This one was obviously a newcomer and with school only having started a few days ago, she'd not had a chance to acquaint herself with the new students.

"I see. So have you lost your way around the building?" she asked then gestured down the empty corridor. "The exit door to the parking area is at the opposite end of this hallway and around the corner."

Shaking his head, he gave her another confident grin. "I'm not lost. I'm waiting on my dad and brother to come pick me up."

Stacy discreetly glanced at the watch on her wrist. Apparently, something had happened to cause the child's father to be late.

"Your father must be running late. Everyone will be leaving the building pretty soon and I wouldn't want you to have to stand outside alone," she told him.

The boy didn't appear to be the least bit concerned over the prospect.

He said, "Oh, it's not unusual for Dad to be late. See, he's the new agribusiness teacher at Bronco High School and that makes him super busy. 'Cause ag teachers have all kinds of extra things they gotta do. He'll be here any minute. I'm not worried."

She'd not heard about the school district hiring a new agribusiness teacher. But that was hardly surprising. With Stacy working at the elementary school there were plenty of matters regarding the high school that she never heard about.

"Most teachers are very busy and I'm sure your father has plenty to do," she replied while wondering about Oliver's mother. Apparently, the woman's schedule made it impossible for her to pick up her son from school.

"My dad's name is Winston Jackson, but everybody calls him Win. And my brother's name is Joshua. He's fifteen and in ninth grade." A smirk twisted his young features. "Joshua thinks he's cool now because he's in high school. But I can't see he's any different than he was this summer."

Stacy kept her smile to herself. She knew firsthand what it was like to have older siblings. Being petite in stature and the baby of the family, she'd often been referred to as the runt. Most of the time the teasing hadn't bothered her, but there had been occasions it had hurt.

"You know something, Oliver? Being a fourth grader is just as important as being a ninth grader. I imagine you're about ten now. Right?"

Clearly impressed that she'd guessed his age, he said, "Yeah. How did you know?"

"Well, usually fourth graders are ten or somewhere close to it," she explained.

He shifted his weight from one foot to the other and Stacy noticed the boy was wearing a pair of brown cowboy boots. The heels were the Western-slanted kind and the snub toes were scuffed. Oliver clearly wasn't the athletic shoe type, she mused silently.

"Are you married?" he asked frankly.

Accustomed to young children asking personal questions, she gave him an indulgent smile. "No. I'm single."

Surprise widened his green eyes. "What about kids? I bet you have kids."

"I don't have children of my own, but I consider my students as my children," she told him.

"That's not the same," he pointed out then swiped at the hank of hair pestering his eye. "My mother died when

I was only three. I don't remember her. But I've seen pictures of her."

Several scenarios had already gone through Stacy's head about the mother of the Jackson family, but none had included the woman being deceased. The information caught her completely off guard. "I'm very sorry to hear that, Oliver. Then it's only you and your brother and father living at home?"

"Yeah. Just us three," he answered and then promptly asked, "Do you have a mother and dad?"

"Yes. They own the Bonnie B Ranch. That's where I live—on the ranch in a cabin of my own."

The word *ranch* caused his eyes to suddenly sparkle. "I live on a ranch, too! Dad's named it the J Barb. He bought the place when we moved here a few months back. It's not all built yet, but it's gonna be good. We already have cattle and horses. But Dad is planning on buying lots more. He says you gotta have plenty of livestock to make money."

So apparently the Jackson family hadn't always lived in the Bronco area, she thought. But investing in ranching property implied the new agribusiness teacher was planning on staying permanently.

"That's true," she said, asking, "Do you like living on a ranch?"

A look of comical confusion swept over his face. "Gee, doesn't everybody? It's great. We've always lived on a ranch. Living in town wouldn't be fun. Back in Whitehorn, I had friends who lived in town and they had to follow rules that were just awful. When we played in the yard we couldn't yell 'cause the neighbor didn't like kids yelling. And they couldn't let their dogs out of the backyard. That was sad. 'Cause dogs like to run and explore."

"Town life is different," she agreed. "But not everyone is fortunate enough to live on a ranch."

"That's what Dad says. And he says land costs too darn much. That's why we have to take care of it."

Sounded as though Winston Jackson was teaching his boys to be good stewards of the land, she reasoned. That meant he was probably a wonderful agriculture teacher.

Oliver glanced down the hallway at the same time Stacy caught the sound of footsteps thumping against the tiled floor.

She followed the boy's gaze and instantly caught sight of a tall man wearing a gray cowboy hat and black boots. His long legs were taking purposeful strides straight toward them and just as Stacy was thinking he had to be Winston Jackson, Oliver declared, "There's Dad! Come on, Ms. Abernathy! I want you to meet him!"

Oliver scurried off and, not wanting to appear unfriendly, Stacy followed at a sedate pace until the three of them met in the middle of the wide corridor.

Standing proudly at his father's side, Oliver quickly made introductions. "Dad, this is Ms. Abernathy. She teaches second grade. We've been ranch talking. She lives on a ranch, too. The Bonnie B."

The moment Oliver's father had walked up to them, Stacy had felt herself gawking at the man and now, as he extended his hand to greet her, she felt a wash of heat sting her cheeks.

"Nice to meet you, Ms. Abernathy. I'm Winston Jackson—just call me Win. I hope Oliver hasn't been talking your ear off. In case you haven't already guessed, talking is his best subject."

The man was a dream in the form of a cowboy. Well over six feet with broad, muscular shoulders and dirty-blond hair that waved around his ears and slightly onto the back of his neck. He was wearing dark trousers, a pale blue Western shirt and a bolo tie with a slide fashioned from a malachite stone. The green color matched his eyes, she thought and then immediately wondered why in the world she'd be noticing something so insignificant about Win Jackson.

"It's nice to meet you, Win. And please, call me Stacy—everyone does—except for the students, of course."

Those deep green eyes met hers and Stacy felt certain her heart skipped a beat or two. The strong reaction caught her by surprise. She was accustomed to seeing good-looking cowboys around town. After all, Bronco was full of them. But she'd never met one that struck her as hard as this one. Or could it be her erratic pulse was simply trying to tell her she'd gone without a date for far too long?

Thankfully, Oliver suddenly spoke up and interrupted her silly thoughts.

"Aww, shoot. Guess that means I have to keep calling you Ms. Abernathy," he said.

Stacy gave the boy an indulgent smile. "I'm afraid so, Oliver. If the other students heard you calling me Stacy, it would cause problems. Because here at school I'm Ms. Abernathy, the teacher. Do you understand?"

She looked over to see Win was running a quick gaze over her face and Stacy decided it wasn't the sort of look a man gave a woman when he was romantically interested. Instead, he appeared to be summing her up as a teacher and nothing more.

"Since I'm a teacher, Oliver gets to thinking he can get personal with other teachers. I'll make sure he remembers you're Ms. Abernathy," he said.

"I won't forget and slip," Oliver told her, then looked up

at his father and added, "Ms. Abernathy isn't married. She doesn't have any kids, either."

Win scowled at his son. "Oliver, how many times have I told you not to be asking people personal questions? All of those things are Ms. Abernathy's private business, not yours."

Seeing a dejected look come over the boy's face, Stacy quickly spoke up with a little laugh, "Oh, it's okay, Win. I've lived in Bronco all my life. Everyone around here knows everything there is to know about me. Half of them could probably tell you what I ate for lunch."

Her attempt to joke didn't produce a chuckle from Win, but it did put a faint smile on his face.

"Thanks for being understanding about my son's nosiness," he said.

A nervous tickle suddenly struck her throat but she refused to clear it away. The last thing she wanted was for this rugged man to get the idea he was making her feel like an awkward teenaged girl.

"Oliver tells me you're teaching agribusiness at the high school. How's your new job going for you?" she asked politely.

"I've taught agribusiness for sixteen years; it's old hat with me. But being at Bronco High School is a new experience. So far, I've not had any problems. Most of the students are obedient and attentive and the school administration has been great."

It was sinful for a man to look as good as him, Stacy thought. He probably had a list of girlfriends as long as his arm.

Pushing that thought aside, she said, "Well, I hope you enjoy living in Bronco, Win. Naturally, I'm biased, but it truly is a great town."

"It's beginning to feel like home to the boys and me," he said, placing a big hand on Oliver's shoulder. "Come along, son. Joshua is waiting and we have lots of chores to do before supper."

Oliver gave her a little wave. "Bye, Ms. Abernathy. Maybe I'll see you here in the hallway tomorrow."

Stacy gave the boy a nod. "You certainly might."

"Good meeting you." Win tossed the pleasantry at her before hurriedly bustling Oliver down the hallway.

Stacy watched the father and son until they reached the end of the corridor and disappeared around the corner. As she turned to walk back to her room, she couldn't help thinking Win Jackson was certainly a hot hunk of cowboy, but he hadn't seemed overly sociable.

And why would he be extra sociable with you, Stacy? You're not exactly a glamour girl and, from the looks of the man, he can have his pick of women.

The mocking voice bouncing around in her head was suddenly interrupted by two female voices directly behind her. Turning, she saw Emma Garner, the first-grade teacher and teacher's aide, Carrie Waters.

"Stacy! Who the heck was that?" Emma asked.

"I think I need to turn on the air conditioner!" Carrie exclaimed as she used one hand to fan her face. "It's way too hot in here!"

Trying her best to appear cool and casual, Stacy said, "That was Win Jackson. He's the new agribusiness teacher over at Bronco High."

Carrie, a redhead who was all for having a night of fun, released a wistful sigh. "Oh my. He's a dream in cowboy boots! But I'll bet he's married. The ones who look that good always are."

Emma rolled her eyes. "The ones who look that good are always trouble—whether they're married or not."

Stacy said, "Win is a widower. That was his son, Oliver, with him. He also has an older son in high school."

"A widower," Carrie repeated soberly. "That's terrible. Those poor boys."

"I'd say poor Win, too," Emma added thoughtfully. "To be a widower so young—I can't imagine going through that kind of pain."

"I can't imagine it, either," Stacy replied. "Losing his wife and the mother of his children had to be heartbreaking."

"Wonder how long he's been a widower?" Carrie thoughtfully voiced the question then looked to Stacy for an answer.

Stacy's first instinct was to tell Carrie she had no idea how long it had been since Mrs. Jackson had passed away. The information was Win's personal and private business. On the other hand, it was hardly a secret. Not with a talkative son like Oliver.

"From what Oliver told me, his mother has been gone seven years. Since he was three years old. He says he doesn't remember her."

"Heartbreaking," Emma murmured. "I wonder if Mr. Jackson ever thinks his boys might need a mother in their lives?"

Stacy had been wondering the same thing, but she wasn't going to admit it to her coworkers. Both women were often suggesting that she needed to date more. She didn't want either of them to latch onto the idea that she might be interested in Win Jackson.

"Possibly," she answered Emma's question. "But he's been single for a long time. It doesn't look like he wants another wife or a stepmother for his sons."

"What a waste," Carrie replied.

"Everyone deals with loss differently," Emma said with a rueful grimace. "And some people only have it in them to love once in a lifetime."

Was Win Jackson in that category? Stacy wondered. Had he already used up all his romantic love on his late wife? The idea was disturbing. She would think a man like him would be full of needs and passion. But then, what did she know about a hot romance? Her limited encounters with men could be labeled lukewarm to cold, she rationalized ruefully.

Deciding it was time to change the subject, Stacy pointedly checked her watch. "Oh my, it's getting late. I need to collect my things and head home."

Minutes later, as Stacy drove away from the school parking lot and steered her little sedan in the direction of the Bonnie B, she tried not to think about Win Jackson. She even turned up the radio volume in hopes the blasting music would push his image from her mind. But it didn't work. She kept seeing his rugged features with his faint crook of a smile and the calloused feel of his big hand as it had wrapped around hers. Oh, he was all man and then some. Just looking at him had filled her stomach with butterflies.

Yet the image of his sexy good looks wasn't the only thing about Win going through her mind. She kept picturing him and his boys going home to an empty house, with only the three of them sharing dinner. In comparison, it almost made her feel guilty to be heading home to eat dinner with her parents and most likely a sibling or two.

But did that make her more fortunate than Win? At least, he'd been deeply in love once. He'd experienced marriage and, most of all, he had two sons. She didn't even have a steady boyfriend. Maybe she should worry about her own love life instead of Win Jackson's.

Two days later, Win stood in front of his desk as he presented questions to the class of twenty-two sophomores. It was the last hour of the school day and usually by now most of the students were too busy thinking about the bell ringing and what they were planning to do later that night than to focus on learning. That often created a challenge for Win to hold their attention throughout the hour. But this particular group was actually showing interest and he was making the most of the last few minutes.

"Okay, here is your next question. If a cattle rancher is hit by a drought that wipes out his hay crop, would it be more profitable for him to sell his herd and wait for his hay meadows to grow again before he restocks, or to purchase high-priced hay from another source and try to hang on to his cattle?"

Sitting at the back of the room, a girl with short brown hair was the first to thrust her arm in the air.

Win quickly acknowledged her. "Okay, Bethann, tell us how you'd handle this situation in the most profitable way."

The girl said, "Well, Mr. Jackson, the answer will depend on the market price for cattle at the time of the drought. If the market is flooded and the rancher takes a huge loss at the sale barn, then purchasing the high-priced hay would be the best way to go. That's the way I see it."

"You are correct," Win told her. "It all comes down to market prices. Not only for the cattle but also for the hay."

A tall blond boy seated two desks away from Bethann let out a loud groan. "Aww, Bethann knew the answer 'cause her dad works on a ranch. How's the rest of us supposed to know these things?"

"I knew the answer because I use my brain to think, Ralphy," Bethann shot back at her classmate.

Win held up his hand to ward off the chuckles erupting around the room. "The answers were all right there in the two chapters you were assigned to read last night," Win told the boy. "You don't have to have a friend or relative in the ranching business to learn about ranch management. That's why I'm here. To teach you."

"Yes, sir," Ralphy meekly replied. "I understand."

Win glanced down at the notes he was holding, but not before he saw Ralphy send Bethann a sheepish grin that turned her cheeks a shade of pink. The exchange had Win remembering his days in high school and the juvenile attempts he'd made at flirting with the girls. That time in his life was long past and since Yvette's death, he'd had no desire to flirt with any woman.

Until last night, he reminded himself. Until he'd walked upon Stacy Abernathy.

Nearly two days had passed since he'd met the second-grade teacher, yet her image was still far too fresh in his mind. Sparkling blue eyes, smooth ivory skin surrounded by golden-blond hair, lips the color of crushed strawberries. She'd been lovely and, for the first time in a long time, he'd noticed.

Damn it! He wasn't in the market for romance. Other than her being pretty, he didn't know why he was still thinking about the woman. Hadn't he learned his lesson back in Whitehorn?

Purposely shaking that mocking question aside, he focused on the notes in his hand and was about to present another question to the class when the loud buzz of the bell interrupted his plans and he quickly dismissed the class.

As the students gathered up books and supplies and hurriedly filed out of the room, Win rounded his desk and began shoving a stack of test papers to be graded into a brown canvas duffel bag.

"Hey, Win. You haven't forgotten about the meeting tonight, have you?"

Win glanced over at the open doorway to see Anthony Landers, Bronco High's phys ed teacher and baseball coach. In his late twenties, with a head full of curly black hair and a constant grin, he was a likable guy, plus a hard worker. He had quickly grown into Win's best friend in Bronco.

"Meeting? I guess I have. What sort of meeting?"

Entering the room Anthony pulled a folded paper from his back pocket and handed it to Win. "Didn't you get an email about the meeting? I made a print of mine."

Win quickly scanned the message then cursed under his breath. The meeting started at six tonight. That would hardly give him enough time to collect the boys, drive out to the J Barb, do the evening chores and then drive back into Bronco.

Handing the note back to Anthony, he shook his head. "If I did, I don't remember it. Now I've got to figure out what to do with the boys while I'm at the meeting."

"Oh, that's easy enough. I'm leaving the gym open so any of the teachers' kids can play basketball or volleyball while we're at the meeting."

Win let out a mocking laugh. "And who's going to keep the kids from cutting the nets off the goals or scarring up the floor with hard shoes? Teachers' kids aren't always angels, you know. My two boys included."

Anthony laughed. "Your boys are well mannered. No worries, though. A couple of teacher's aides have volunteered to oversee things until the meeting is finished."

"Thanks for letting me know, Anthony. I'll send the boys

to the gym. Do you have any idea how long these meetings last?"

"Usually not more than an hour or so. Just long enough to make you good and starved by the time you get home."

"Yeah," Win said wryly. "Joshua and Oliver will be complaining that they're about to collapse from starvation."

Anthony chuckled. "You'd probably have time to take them out for a quick bite to eat before the meeting. I'd go with you, but I have some extra things to do in the gym."

Win shook his head. "I let them eat fast food last night. I don't want them to have it two nights in a row."

"Oh, to be a father. I'm glad I'm not there yet," Anthony joked before turning to start out of the room. "I'll see you at the meeting."

The young man was about to disappear through the door when Win called to him. "Do you have another minute, Anthony?"

"Sure. You need a favor?"

Win walked over to where the other man stood. "Thanks, but no. I just have a question for you. Are you acquainted with the Abernathy family?"

Anthony chuckled. "That's a mighty broad question, Win. The Abernathys are one of the oldest and richest families in the area. There are dozens of them around here, but I'm only slightly acquainted with them. They're sort of out of my league, if you get my drift."

"You mean because they're rich? Are they snobby?" Win arched a brow at him while thinking Stacy Abernathy hardly came across as a woman with her nose stuck up in the air.

"Not the ones I've been around. Actually they're all pretty down to earth. But—" He paused and shrugged. "I guess being around wealth reminds me of my own meager bank account. Anyway, why are you asking about the Abernathys? Do you have one as a student?"

Win felt like an idiot. "No. I met a teacher over at Oliver's school by the name of Stacy Abernathy. I was just wondering about her—'cause Oliver seems to be overly taken with her."

Anthony frowned thoughtfully then nodded. "Yeah. I've seen her at a few school events. She's from the Bonnie B bunch of Abernathys. The youngest of the family, I think. She always came across as the quiet type to me. But then, I only know her casually. Mostly through school events. I'm more acquainted with her brothers since I run into them at Doug's bar and other places around town. They're all good guys."

It didn't sound as though the Abernathys put themselves above everyone else. But that didn't mean he should be daydreaming about the pretty blonde teacher, Win told himself. "Well, you know Oliver, he can make anyone talk," he said jokingly.

"Uh, is Oliver in Stacy's class this school year?"

Win glanced over to see Anthony eyeing him with a curious look. "No. She teaches second grade."

"Oh. Well, Oliver probably won't have much contact with her then," Anthony replied. "If that's what's worrying you—him getting too attached to a teacher as a mother figure."

Grimacing, Win turned toward his desk and picked up his duffel bag. Oliver often asked if he'd ever have a mother, and Joshua, when he wasn't trying to be cool, admitted he missed his mother and wished she was with them. Win understood it was a tough situation for both boys, but he couldn't bring Yvette back. And he sure as heck wasn't going to marry just to give his sons a stepmom.

Holding back a heavy sigh, Win said, "I'm not worried. But sometimes I wish he'd be more like Joshua."

"And steer clear of females completely?" Anthony asked then laughed. "Sorry, Win. But I figure both your boys will make the most of their dating years."

Win groaned at the thought. "You're probably right. I might as well get ready for my sons to have their hearts broken a few times."

"It's a part of a young man's growing pains," Anthony replied. "At least, that's what my dad always told me."

Yeah, Win thought grimly. A man learned about falling in love. Then he had to learn all about losing it. As far as he was concerned, he'd had all the love lessons he could stand in a lifetime.

"So how does it feel having Joshua in your freshman ag class? I can't imagine having my own child as a student."

Win flashed him a pointed grin. "It's not always easy trying to walk the fine line between teacher and father. But so far things have been going okay," he said, then deliberately glanced at his wristwatch. "We'd better get going."

"Right. Or I'll be late for the meeting."

The two men left the room together and, after parting company in the hallway, Win hurried out to his truck. With any luck, he could get to the elementary school and collect Oliver without running into Ms. Stacy Abernathy a second time.

The pretty blond teacher had made him uncomfortable in a way he'd not felt in years. He didn't need that kind of temptation. Or the reminder that the days of him having a woman in his life were long over.

Chapter Two

As Stacy entered the Bronco High School building and found her way to the conference room, she was feeling a bit of nerves about attending the district meeting. And that was a ridiculous reaction. She'd been to these workshop-type meetings dozens of times. Mostly, she'd ended up being bored with hearing the same old motivational talks about keeping the students focused on their lessons and eager to learn.

But she needed to be honest with herself. Nothing about the meeting was causing her stomach to flutter and her palms to grow damp. What was really on her mind was the idea of seeing Win Jackson again. Would he notice her? And if he did, would he bother to acknowledge her?

Pausing in the hallway, outside the closed door of the conference room, Stacy took a moment to glance down at the brown suede midi skirt and waist-length pumpkin-colored sweater she'd changed into before she'd driven here to the high school. The pieces weren't exactly glamour-girl attire, but if Win did glance her way, he might think she looked nice.

Nice. Is that the best you can do, Stacy? If you want to catch the eye of that hunky cowboy, then you're going to have to do better than nice!

Shaking away the annoying voice in her head, Stacy entered the meeting room to find most of the teachers had arrived, with many of them already taking up seats at the rows of long utility tables. The administrative staff was gathered at a table near the podium at the head of the room. She spotted the principal of Bronco Elementary along with the assistant superintendent, comparing notes, while near the podium an older man was setting up a projector screen.

She was casting her gaze around the room, searching for an empty chair, when she spotted Emma waving to catch her attention. Stacy made her way over to her friend and sank into the folding chair next to her.

Emma leaned her head close to Stacy's and spoke in a lowered voice. "I was beginning to wonder if you were going to get here. It's almost time for the meeting to start."

Stacy blew out a weary breath. "I had to go home to change clothes because my dress got streaked with mud during recess. Seven-year-olds forget about putting dirty hands where they don't belong. Anyway, I think I broke the speed limit on the way back to town. Thankfully, I didn't get pulled over."

"You speeding? I'd never believe you'd do anything that... reckless. Especially for a change of clothes." Emma rolled her eyes and chuckled. "But you do look pretty tonight."

"Thanks. I was afraid you were going to say I look nice."

Emma's brows lifted. "What's wrong with looking nice?"

Because being a step above ordinary would never catch Win Jackson's attention, Stacy thought, immediately wishing she could kick herself. This sudden infatuation she'd developed over a man she'd spoken to for less than three minutes was ridiculous and she needed to stop it. Now!

"Not a thing," Stacy replied. "Nice is better than homely."

Emma grunted with humor. "You, homely? You can be

so funny at times, Stacy. And speaking of looking good, I see the hunky ag teacher just walked into the room. Too bad there's not an empty chair at our table. He might've joined us."

"I doubt it." Stacy steeled herself not to turn her head and stare, but found it impossible to keep from slanting a look from the corner of her eye.

Taller than she remembered and dressed in black Western-cut slacks and a gray shirt, Win Jackson carried his black Stetson in one hand as he made his way to a table where several male teachers were seated. He sank into an empty chair next to Anthony Landers and, from the way the two men greeted each other, it was clear they'd become friends. The notion had her wondering who else the man might've made friends with since moving to Bronco. Some of the young female teachers at Bronco High? Or some of the women he'd encountered around town?

Her thoughts about the man were on the verge of spinning out of control when he suddenly looked up and straight at her. He didn't smile or nod or acknowledge her in any way, yet when their gazes clashed, Stacy was certain she'd seen a flash of recognition in his eyes.

"Looks like things are finally going to get started," Emma mumbled under her breath. "It's about time, don't you think?"

Stacy jerked her gaze away from Win Jackson to stare blankly at Emma. "About time? For what?"

Emma rolled her eyes. "Stacy, that hurried trip you made to the Bonnie B to change clothes must have scattered your senses. I'm talking about the meeting getting started. What else?"

Feeling like a complete fool, Stacy blew out a long breath. "Oh—yes. The meeting. Sorry, Emma, my day has been hectic from the moment I got up, and I have a dozen different things on my mind."

Like one tall cowboy with wavy blond hair and green eyes. Right, Stacy?

Thankfully, the mocking voice in Stacy's head was drowned out as Leonard Mangrum, superintendent of the school district, suddenly spoke into the microphone.

"Good evening, everyone. I'm happy to see all you dedicated teachers here tonight. I hope..."

The rest of the man's words were lost on Stacy as she glanced discreetly over at Win's table. Expecting him to be focused on Leonard, she was shocked to see he was looking straight at her. Again. Was it possible he might be interested? Maybe, just maybe, after the meeting ended, he'd come over to say hello.

After long years of teaching, Win would rather count the horn flies on a bull's back than sit through a workshop. But it was a part of the job and, frankly, he loved teaching. The profession was rarely easy, but it was always rewarding to see his students grow into productive adults. Still, he wished tonight he was sitting anywhere but directly across the room from Stacy Abernathy. Fate was definitely trying to tempt or torment him, he lamented. Each time he glanced over at her, he was struck with a strange sense of connection. He barely knew the woman. How could that be?

Win was deep in thought, attempting to answer the self-imposed question when Anthony's elbow gouged into his rib cage.

"Hey, Win. Wake up. The meeting has ended."

Anthony's voice jarred him back to the present and he looked around to see most of the crowd heading toward the door. Embarrassed that he'd been caught daydreaming, he snatched up his hat and crammed it onto his head.

"I knew the meeting was over. I was…thinking about something."

"Ha! Don't try to fool me. You were about to fall asleep."

Relieved that his friend hadn't noticed he was actually woolgathering, he joked, "After that last motivational talk, can you blame me? Come on, let's go see if the gym has been demolished."

Five minutes later, after Win collected Oliver and Joshua from the gymnasium, the three of them walked to the designated teachers section of the parking lot. Win's black four-door truck was parked in the middle of the back row and as soon as it came into view, the boys took off in a trot toward the waiting vehicle.

Win punched the key fob to unlock the doors and by the time he climbed in the driver's seat, the boys were already strapped securely inside their seat belts.

"I'm starving, Dad," Joshua said. "Are we going by the burger place before we go home?"

"No! Let's get fried chicken and gravy!" Oliver spoke up. "We have burgers all the time!"

"That's because burgers are better than chicken," Joshua argued. "Especially with cheese fries."

"Sorry, boys, we're not going to eat fast food tonight." He clicked in his own seat belt before glancing over his shoulder. Both his sons looked disappointed. "I'll fix something when we get home. There's plenty of leftover stew. How does that sound?"

Joshua groaned out a protest while Oliver clapped in agreement.

"I'm all for stew. I like it," he said, leaning forward to be closer to his father's seat. "Dad, did you see Ms. Abernathy at the meeting tonight?"

Win frowned as he stuck the key into the ignition. He should've expected Oliver to question him about the pretty blonde. He'd brought her name up several times in the past couple of days and Win was beginning to wonder if Anthony might've touched on something when he'd suggested Oliver might be getting attached to Stacy as a mother figure.

"Yes," Win answered. "I saw her sitting across the room."

"Gosh, I'll bet she looked pretty," Oliver said in an excited rush. "Did you get to talk to her?"

Win had thought long and hard about talking to her. He'd even considered going over to her after the meeting and inviting her out for a cup of coffee. With the boys accompanying them, it would've been a harmless enough outing. But then he'd remembered how he'd thought one casual outing with Tara wouldn't hurt anything. Instead, she'd turned into a villain from a badly written horror movie.

"No. The meeting was long and everyone was in a rush to leave," Win told him, thinking he wasn't really stretching the truth. Once the workshop had ended, almost everyone in the room had darted toward the exit.

Oliver said, "Well, you should've talked to her, Dad. She's really nice. You'd like her."

From his side of the seat, Joshua let out a derisive snort. "Oliver, you're so goofy. Dad doesn't need a woman. They're nothing but trouble."

Oliver glared at his big brother. "How do you know? You're just a kid like me!"

Win started the engine. "That's enough, boys."

Ignoring his father's warning, Joshua blasted back at his little brother. "I'm not a kid! I'm fifteen!"

"That's still a kid, too! And I know women aren't bad. You're the one who's goofy! You—"

The contentious bickering between the boys was suddenly lost on Win as he started to back out of the parking space and spotted a woman at the far end of the parking lot lifting the hood of her car.

"Oliver? Do you know what kind of car Ms. Abernathy drives? That looks like her over there."

Win's question quickly put a stop to his sons' argument and Oliver peered out the passenger window to follow his father's gaze.

"Yeah! That's Ms. Abernathy's car. It's little and white. And that's her! She must be having trouble, Dad. You'd better go help her."

Just when he'd been telling himself that he should avoid her and temptation, this happens, he thought wryly.

Reaching for the door latch, he said, "You're right, son. We can't leave Ms. Abernathy stranded."

"Why not?" Joshua mumbled. "The lady must have a cell phone. She can call a garage. And I'm hungry."

Win slanted his son a look of warning. "Right now, I'm going to pretend I didn't hear you say what you just said. But when we get home, you and I are going to have a talk."

Joshua grimaced then dropped his head and mumbled, "Okay. I guess I wasn't being very nice."

Oliver turned a sneer on his brother. "You don't know how to be nice, Joshua!"

This was not the way Win wanted to spend the evening—with two quarreling kids and a woman who made him itch in all the wrong places.

"Dad, Oliver is being a brat and—"

Win quickly interrupted. "No more arguing out of either of you."

Oliver turned a pleading look at his father. "I don't want to stay here with Joshua. Can I go with you, Dad?"

Win realized Oliver's request was more about seeing Stacy Abernathy rather than getting away from his wise-cracking brother.

"All right," Win told him. "As long as you stay out of the way."

Stacy had never considered herself a mechanic, how-ever her father and brothers had taught her a few basics about the workings of a vehicle, just in case she had trou-ble on the road. And unfortunately tonight she was having trouble. She wasn't exactly sure why her car was refusing to start, but before she called one of her brothers for help, she'd make an effort to fix the problem herself.

Pulling on her jacket, she exited the car and lifted the hood. After a quick glance to make sure no wires were hanging lose, she turned her attention to the battery. She was checking the cables to make sure they were secure and making contact when a male voice called to her.

"Need some help?"

Turning, she was totally surprised to see Win and Oli-ver striding up to her. After the way he'd hurriedly left the conference room without a word to anyone, she wouldn't have expected him to still be on the school grounds.

Stepping away from the car, she met the pair on the middle of the concrete walkway that ran adjacent to the parking spaces. "I'm not sure if my battery is dead or if there's some other problem going on, but the car refuses to start," she explained to Win. "The car was fine when I parked it here before the meeting. Now, it's not making a sound. Not even a click. The gas tank is nearly full, so it didn't run out of fuel."

"I'll have a look." He stepped over to the car and peered beneath the hood.

Stacy and Oliver stood to one side while they waited for Win to finish his inspection.

Turning his back to the vehicle, he asked, "Has the car done this before?"

"No. It's never given me any trouble," she told him. Then, not wanting Oliver to feel ignored, she gave the boy a smile. "How are you, Oliver?"

"I'm good, Ms. Abernathy," Oliver spoke up. "And don't worry. Dad knows how to fix all sorts of things. Even tractors. He'll get you going."

"I wouldn't start making promises, Oliver," Win told his son. "The problem might be something that will require a new part from the auto supply store."

Stacy watched him jiggle a pair of wires then lift the cover on the battery and peer into the three holes on top of the square apparatus.

After putting the cover back in place, he said, "Try to start the car again so I can hear what's going on."

She hurried around to the driver's side of the vehicle and slipped beneath the wheel. When she turned the key in the ignition, there wasn't a sound to be heard.

Climbing out of the car, she went to stand next to him. "Usually when a battery goes dead it will, at least, make a clicking noise. It's not even making that sound."

With an understanding nod, he said, "You're right. But nowadays most batteries don't give you any warning that they're going bad. It just happens all at once without so much as a click. I have jumper cables in my truck. We might be able to jump-start it."

"Are you sure you have time?" she asked. "I imagine you and the boys need to get home."

He slanted her a wry look. "I'm sure you need to get home, too."

"Shoot, Ms. Abernathy, we never know when we're gonna get home," Oliver assured her. "Sometimes it's way past my bedtime."

Win let out a good-natured groan. "Oliver, you're going to have Stacy thinking I'm not a good parent. You know you're usually in bed on time."

Grinning, Oliver scuffed the toe of his boot against the concrete sidewalk. "Yeah, mostly I'm in bed on time."

Stacy smiled at the child then looked at Win. "You need to remember I teach elementary school, Win. I'm used to my students saying anything and everything. Usually how they describe something is far different than how it actually is."

He let out a short laugh. "You're telling me. I never know what's going to come out of Oliver's mouth. Joshua's, either, for that matter," he said, adding, "I'll go get my truck. Hopefully, a jump will get you going."

Five minutes later, with Stacy's battery hooked to Win's, he tried starting the car, but it refused.

"It's determined not to start." Stacy stated the obvious.

"No. I'm afraid you're going to have to call a garage and have a new battery installed."

Even though she wanted to let out a groan of disappointment, she choked it back. Not for anything would she do a bunch of complaining in front of Win. She hardly wanted him to view her as a woman who had childish meltdowns over a minor problem.

"Well, Bronco probably does have a twenty-four-hour garage, but Dad has a certain mechanic he always uses. I'll call him tomorrow and ask him to come do the repairs."

He began unclipping the jumper cables from both batteries. "You'll need a lift home," he said.

"No problem," she assured him. "I'll call my parents, or siblings. One of them will come and pick me up. I can wait right here in the car."

His brows pulled together in a frown. "The night is already getting chilly and you obviously can't run the car heater. I can drive you out to the Bonnie B."

He didn't sound annoyed with the situation. On the other hand, he didn't appear to be all that thrilled about the prospect, either, Stacy thought. That was understandable. He had children to care for and most likely ranching chores to deal with before he retired for the evening. Still, it would've been nice of him to smile when he'd made the offer.

Instinctively raising her chin, she said, "Thanks, but I'll be fine waiting here. This is a safe neighborhood. Besides, I've interrupted your evening enough already."

He glanced at her. "You said that, I didn't."

Oliver suddenly piped up. "Dad, we really should drive Ms. Abernathy home. That's the way guys are supposed to treat ladies. Right?"

"Right, son," he told Oliver then cast a wry smile at Stacy. "If you'll fetch your things from the car and lock it up, we'll be on our way."

To argue further would only make her look ungrateful. Besides, who was she kidding? Spending a few more minutes in Win's company was the most exciting thing that had happened to her since last year when her students had presented her a cake on her twenty-seventh birthday.

"Thank you, Win. I really do appreciate this."

"Forget it," he said. "If I ever get stranded, you can give me a lift."

While Win put the jumper cables away and shut both hoods on the vehicles, Stacy gathered a tote bag filled with books and school papers she was planning to go over later tonight, along with her jacket and handbag.

"I'll carry those things for you, Ms. Abernathy," Oliver offered.

Smiling at the sweet boy, she handed him the tote bag. "Thanks, Oliver. It's not too heavy for you, is it?"

"Gosh no! I can carry a whole bucket of feed easy. Dad says toting feed buckets will build my muscles. Do you help do the chores on the Bonnie B, Ms. Abernathy?" he asked as the two of them made their way around to the front passenger door of the truck.

"Not very often. My brothers do most of the ranch chores."

Her answer put a disappointed look on his face. She supposed Oliver was like most of the folks around Bronco who'd known her since she was a child. Because she'd been born and raised on a ranch, everyone thought she should want to be a cowgirl. However, dealing with livestock had never been her thing. Not that she disliked animals; she loved them. But books and teaching had always been her main passion and she was very thankful her family had understood she'd needed to take a different direction with her life.

Oliver said, "Oh. Well, I guess you being a girl and all, you probably don't want to build muscles."

She wanted to laugh but held the reaction back in fear it might hurt Oliver's feelings. He was such a friendly child and it was obvious he wanted to impress her. Just like most boys wanted to impress their mothers. Except that Oliver and his brother didn't have a mother, she recalled sadly.

"Girls want to have a few muscles and be strong, too," she told the boy.

Oliver looked curiously up at her. "Did you ever play baseball?"

She said, "No. But I've played a little softball."

He appeared to be impressed that she was able to do more than teach school and read books. "That's good. I play Little League. But it's over for the summer."

Oliver placed her tote bag on the floor in front of the passenger seat and Stacy was about to climb into the truck when Win appeared at her side and quickly slipped a hand beneath her elbow.

"I'll help you," he said. "It's a tall step up."

Although it was an innocent touch, the feel of his warm fingers against her arm was enough to send her pulse into a wild gallop.

"Thank you, Win."

"Sure," he replied. "Can you find the seat belt? It's rarely ever used. The boys always sit in the back, so the belt might have slipped between the cracks of the seat."

He was standing so near, she could feel the heat radiating from his body, smell the faint earthy scent emanating from his shirt. She'd never had a man make her hands tremble before, but as she dug around for the seat belt, she realized hers were shaking. Hopefully, the semidarkness of the parking lot made it impossible for him to see her fumbling fingers.

"Uh, here it is. I have it."

Satisfied that she was all set, he shut the door and promptly instructed Oliver to join Joshua, who'd been waiting in the back seat all this time.

When Win slid behind the wheel and started the engine, Stacy felt as if the interior of the truck had shrunk to half its size. The man's masculine presence was overwhelming and even though she wasn't looking at him directly, she was totally aware of his long, lean body, the scent of his skin, and the flex of his shoulders as he steered the vehicle out of the parking lot.

"Stacy, I don't think you've met my older son yet," he said, glancing back over his shoulder to the teenager. "Joshua, say hello to Ms. Abernathy. She teaches second grade at the elementary school."

Twisting around in the seat, Stacy looked around the headrest to greet the older boy. "Hello, Joshua. It's nice to meet you."

"Hi."

The one word was all he said, and Stacy wondered if the teenager was usually this quiet or if he was shy.

"We're going to take Ms. Abernathy home. She lives on the Bonnie B Ranch," Win explained to his older son.

"Oh. Where is that?" Joshua asked.

"About ten miles from our ranch," Win answered.

Joshua didn't say anything after that and Stacy got the feeling the boy was pouting about something. His dad helping a woman? Or her making them late getting home?

"Don't pay any attention to Joshua being so quiet, Ms. Abernathy," Oliver told her. "He doesn't know how to talk to women. Not like I do."

"Shut up, you little jerk," Joshua barked at his brother.

"Then why ain't you talkin'?" Oliver taunted back at him.

"Don't say *ain't*. You know what Dad says about saying *ain't*!"

"You two also know what I say about arguing," Win told the boys. "Especially in front of company. Now, pipe down back there."

Silence ensued and, after a moment, Stacy awkwardly cleared her throat. "Oliver tells me you're in the process of building your ranch. How's that going?"

"I wish I had more hours in the day to do more. But now that school has started—well, as a teacher, you know how limited our time gets. And once it gets dark, there's not much work you can do out of doors. Still, I'm pleased with how it's all going so far. I have a small herd of Black Baldy and a few horses."

"We have cats and dogs, too, Ms. Abernathy," Oliver added. "And a pair of burros to guard the cattle."

"Oh, I imagine they're cute little things," she said.

"They're mean." Joshua spoke up. "They'll bite you if you don't watch them. We've had them for a long time. Even when we lived in Whitehorn. Dad says they're family, so they moved here with us."

"I see," she murmured and then glanced over at Win's dark profile. He appeared to be focused on the highway and the intermittent traffic, but she wondered if he might be thinking back to Whitehorn and the life he'd had there with his late wife. Was his heart still wrapped up in her memory? Was that the reason he'd remained single for so long? If so, he might never want another wife. "What made you decide to move to Bronco?" she asked. "Did you hear it was a good ranching area?"

He shrugged one shoulder. "I was ready for a change and when I researched Bronco, it seemed like a good place to build a ranch and teach school."

"And Dad wanted to leave Whitehorn because of Tara," Oliver added tersely.

"Shut up, Oliver!" Joshua muttered under his breath.

"You're the one who needs to shut up!" Oliver practically shouted.

Win turned a look of warning on the two boys before glancing at Stacy. "I apologize for my sons' behavior, Stacy.

It's probably hard to believe, but they're usually not this un-ruly. I hope you don't think my students are this disruptive."

At the moment, Stacy wasn't thinking about his sons or his students, she was wondering about Tara and what had happened with her and Win. But he clearly wasn't going to explain Oliver's remark and Stacy wasn't about to ask.

Chapter Three

Oliver had his nose pressed to the passenger window as Win drove through the ranch yard and on to the big ranch house.

"Wow! This place is really big!" the boy exclaimed. "Look at that gigantic barn, Joshua!"

"Yeah. It's bigger than ours," Joshua replied. "Is that log mansion where you live, Ms. Abernathy?"

"That's my parents' home. I have a smaller cabin of my own about a half-mile behind this one. But I stay here with my parents fairly often, too."

"Why?" Oliver wanted to know. "Because this place is big and fancy?"

She answered, "It's a big house, but I wouldn't call it a mansion, Oliver. It's not overly fancy—just nice and comfortable. Ever since I was born twenty-eight years ago, this has been my home. And even though I have a place of my own, I stay here often because—well, my parents enjoy my company and I enjoy theirs."

To her, it probably wasn't a mansion, Win thought. But to him and the boys, it was fancy. In fact, from what Win could see about the Bonnie B, everything was bigger and more impressive than most of the places he'd seen around Bronco. That didn't surprise him. Anthony had already told him how the Abernathys were some of the most affluent of families in and around Bronco. And from the looks of this place, he doubted Stacy had ever had to want for anything.

Just one more reason Win needed to keep his distance from the woman, he told himself. Not that he was poor by any means, but his financial status could hardly stand up to that of Stacy's family. And he figured she'd never be the type to lower her standards. Even for love.

Love! Hell, he must've gone too long without eating today, Win wryly chided himself. Otherwise, that word would've never popped into his head.

"Well, here we are," she announced as he pulled the truck to a stop in front of a yard fence made of split rails. "I'd be happy if you'd all come in and have some of Mom's homemade cookies. At least it would be a little repayment for all your trouble."

Win didn't allow himself the time to consider her invitation. No matter how nice she was being and how innocent her offer, he needed to put some distance between the two of them. "Thanks. It sounds very nice, Stacy. But we really should head on to the J Barb."

Oliver immediately let out a loud wail. "Oh, Dad, can't we go in just for a few minutes? We don't ever get to eat homemade cookies! Unless we visit Grandma and Grandpa!"

"I wouldn't mind a few cookies myself," Joshua added.

Seeing both boys were on board for the treat, Win could hardly refuse. Besides, turning down her offer would probably make her see him as an unfriendly jerk. "All right," he conceded. "But we can't stay for very long. Ms. Abernathy has things she needs to do and so do we."

"Yeah! Homemade cookies!" Oliver exclaimed. "This will be good!"

They departed the truck and, with Win carrying Stacy's

tote, she walked along beside him as the two boys followed a few steps behind the adults.

The night was cool with a breeze gently ruffling the leaves that were still clinging to a couple of Aspen trees growing in the far corner of the yard. A multitude of stars dotted the inky sky while a crescent moon was rising on the eastern horizon. In the distance, beyond a group of barns and corrals, he could hear a pair of dogs bark and the sound of bawling cows and calves.

"Sounds like it's weaning time on the Bonnie B," he commented.

She sighed. "Yes. I hate weaning time on the ranch."

Her remark disappointed him. In spite of her not being an outdoor, cowgirl type, he wanted to believe she respected the ranching profession. "Why?" he asked. "The noise gets on your nerves?"

Smiling, sheepishly, she said, "No. It's not that at all. It's because I'm too softhearted, I guess. It's sad to hear the mothers and babies calling so desperately to each other. But Dad says it's a part of life—like kids growing up and leaving the nest, so to speak." She glanced at him. "Do you have calves on the J Barb to wean this fall?"

"I finished separating the cows and calves a couple of weeks ago. I wanted to have it done before school started."

"Do you have hired hands to help on your ranch?" she asked.

Even though her question was a reasonable one, it very nearly made Win laugh. "Yeah. These two guys behind me. They're my helpers." Seeing the faint look of surprise on her face, he went on to explain, "My ranch isn't big enough to support hired help. Especially on a full-time basis. I basically take care of everything that needs to be done, and the boys have been learning how to do things around the ranch since they were very small. They're good help."

"I see. Sounds like my dad and brothers," she said. "Mom says he put them in the saddle when they were toddlers."

They stepped up on a wide-planked porch that ran the entire width of the enormous house. To the left and right of the entrance, there were groups of cushioned furniture, and porch swings were located at both ends. In several spots, pots of yellow, copper and white chrysanthemums grew in huge clay plots. The flowers made it clear there was a woman's touch on the Bonnie B, Win thought. Something that he'd missed since losing his wife.

"My dad was the same way with me and my brother," he said. "And my boys have been riding since they were very small."

"Like father, like son. Right?" she said with a knowing grin.

"Right."

She stepped up to open the door, but before she could reach for the handle, the glass-and-wood panel swung wide to reveal a tall woman with light-colored hair peering at them.

"Oh, Stacy, it's you! I thought I heard a vehicle pull up." Her brows arched with curiosity as she glanced over her daughter's shoulder at Win and the two boys. "I see you brought company home with you."

"Yes. Or I should say, they brought me home. I had car trouble and had to leave it in the parking lot at the high school. So Win kindly offered to bring me home," Stacy quickly explained then gestured to Win. "Mom, this is Win Jackson. He's the new agribusiness teacher at Bronco High School and these are his two sons. Joshua is fifteen and Oliver is ten. You guys, this is my mother, Bonnie Abernathy."

Stacy's mother quickly stepped onto the porch and, with a wide smile, reached for Win's hand. "A pleasure to meet you, Mr. Jackson. It's certainly nice of you to bring Stacy all the way out here to the Bonnie B."

Bonnie's handshake was as strong and confident as the look in her eye, and Win immediately liked her straightforward demeanor. "The pleasure is all mine, Mrs. Abernathy. And just call me Win. I hear Mr. Jackson all day at school."

She chuckled. "I'm sure you do. So, Win it will be."

Gathering his sons in the curve of one arm, he urged them toward the ranching matriarch. "Boys, say hello to Mrs. Abernathy."

"Hello, Mrs. Abernathy," they repeated in perfect unison.

Laughing, she grabbed both children by the hand and pulled them toward the door she'd left standing open. "No need to call me that, boys. Just call me Bonnie. Now, come on in and make yourselves at home. I'll bet you two would like some cookies, wouldn't you?"

Oliver looked totally puzzled. "How did you know that Ms. Abernathy said we could come in and eat cookies?"

Laughing, Bonnie looked back at Stacy and Win and winked. "Oh, I just sort of guessed," she told Oliver. "Baking cookies is something I do pretty often. In fact, I just took some cowboy cookies out of the oven and they're still warm."

"What's a cowboy cookie?" Joshua wanted to know.

Bonnie's indulgent smile encompassed both boys. "Oh my goodness, a cowboy cookie is just stuffed with yummy things like chocolate chips and nuts and coconut, and a few more things. I think you'll like them."

"I know I will!" Oliver exclaimed.

Curving an arm around both boys' shoulders, her mother

ushered them into the house, leaving Stacy and Win to follow the trio into a short foyer.

"You guys come along with me to the kitchen," Bonnie said to the children and then darted a glance at Win
and her daughter. "Stacy, why don't you show Win to the
den where he can relax while the boys have their cookies.
And, don't worry, Win, I won't let them spoil their appe-
tites. After all, I'm expecting the three of you to stay for
dinner. I promise I've cooked enough to feed an army. Or
have you three already had your dinner?"

The woman's sudden invitation took Win by surprise
and he glanced uncertainly at Stacy. But she merely smiled
at him as though to say she wasn't going to argue his case
for him.

To Bonnie, he said, "No. We've not eaten yet. And it's
very thoughtful of you invite us to stay. But I wouldn't
want to intrude. I'll fix Joshua and Oliver something when
we get home."

"Nonsense! Even with three extra mouths to feed, I'll
have leftovers to deal with. I won't hear of you leaving without dinner. Especially after the trouble you've taken to help
Stacy get home."

The woman was being especially warm and welcoming
and Win certainly appreciated her kindness. Yet he was
barely acquainted with Stacy and had never met any of the
Abernathys. To be thrust into a family situation like this,
especially without any warning, was making him darned
uncomfortable.

"Bonnie, I honestly don't need any sort of repayment
for helping Stacy and—"

"No arguments," she firmly interrupted. "You and your
sons have to eat. You might as well do it here with us.

Stacy, fix him a nice drink. Dinner should be ready in about thirty minutes."

She hurried away with the boys and Stacy gave him an apologetic smile. "Look, Win, I can see you aren't keen on staying for dinner. But you'd be making my parents happy. And my family is fairly easygoing. We usually don't have loud arguments at the dinner table. Plus, Mom is a wonderful cook. Everything she makes is mouthwatering."

"I'm not worried about your mother's cooking skills. I—" He broke off as it struck him that any excuse he made to skip dinner would make him sound as though he was desperate to hightail it out of this log mansion, which he was. But he didn't want to hurt Stacy's feelings. Even if it meant him being miserable for an hour or so. "I appreciate Bonnie inviting us."

A tiny smile tilted the corners of her plush lips and Win suddenly wondered if she'd ever kissed a man with heedless abandon or experienced real passion in a man's arms. From what little time he'd spent in her company, he'd gotten the impression that she was reserved, not anything close to reckless. Yet, at the same time, she had a sweet sexiness about her that made every male cell in his body hum with pleasure.

"I'm glad," she said. "I'd very much appreciate your company."

Her words alone were not that suggestive, but the soft tone in which she'd said them rippled down his spine like the seductive trail of a fingertip. How the heck was he supposed to reply? Out of politeness, he could say it was a nice opportunity for him to get to know her better. But damn it, she might end up being just like Tara—reading more into his words than he'd meant.

Clearing an awkward lump from his throat, he said,

"You're probably going to find my company boring, Stacy. My life is mundane."

With a soft chuckle, she stepped closer and motioned him forward. "A teacher's life is never boring or mundane. If it is, then he or she isn't doing their job," she said as they moved out of the foyer. "Come on, I'll show you to the den."

They entered a grand-sized room with high ceilings, polished wood floors and a row of windows facing the north. Win missed most of the details about the formal living area. He was too busy focused on her soft scent swirling around him and the way the folds of her brown skirt were brushing against his leg.

Several months had passed since a woman's body had been close enough to touch his, even in the most innocuous way. And for the most part, he could easily say he'd not missed the stress of dating and trying to dodge the marriage traps that had been constantly thrown in his direction. In fact, he'd pretty much convinced himself that he could do without a woman's charms indefinitely. But being this close to Stacy was making him rethink his plans to remain celibate the rest of his life.

"This is a huge house," he commented as they walked down a long hallway. "You must have several siblings or your parents simply like plenty of living space."

She smiled at him. "I have four siblings. Three brothers and a sister. I'm the youngest of the bunch and the only one who often stays here in the big house. My sister lives with her husband nearby on the Broken Road Ranch. All the others have cabins of their own on the Bonnie B, which gives them privacy while still remaining close."

He glanced at her. "Guess your frequent stays here in the main house means you don't need extra privacy."

She shrugged. "Well, I'm not married or engaged, like

my siblings," she explained. "And besides, my parents don't hover over me. I'm busy. They're busy. We all stay out of each other's way. Unless we want to be together, of course."

They reached an open doorway where she guided him into a long, rectangular-shaped room furnished with three couches and several armchairs all done in various shades of green and brown leather. At the far end of the room, a small fire was burning in a wide, native-rock fireplace. Other than the crackle of the burning logs, the room was quiet, but Win had a feeling it wouldn't be staying that way for long.

"Here we are," she announced once they reached the center of the room. "Sit wherever you'd like. You might find it more pleasant down by the fire. This room can get drafty at times. Especially when it's breezy outside."

He crossed the room to where a couch was angled toward the fireplace but still far enough away to keep from being roasted. After sinking onto an end cushion, he pulled off his hat and hung it over one knee.

A few feet away, she went behind a short bar and pulled out a yellow-and-green-enameled tray. "What would you like to drink?" she asked. "Something with alcohol? I don't fancy myself as a bartender, but I can mix a few simple drinks."

"Uh, no thanks. I'll be driving myself and the kids home in a bit."

"Good thinking," she said. "So, how about a soda? Ginger ale? Or juice?"

"I'm not choosy. I'll have whatever you're having," he told her.

"Coming right up," she said.

Short minutes later, she appeared in front of him carrying a tray with two glasses filled with crushed ice and some sort of yellow-orange liquid, garnished with a slice of lime.

"Looks good. Thanks," he told her as he picked up one of the glasses.

She placed the tray on an end table then carried her glass over to the middle of the couch and took a seat a couple of cushions down from him.

After she'd watched him take a sip of his drink, she said, "Don't ask me what you're drinking. Some sort of fizzy fruit juice. Mom special orders it. She and Dad went on vacation to Spain several years ago and she says this drink reminds her of their time there."

"It's nice. I like it," he said then slanted a curious glance at her. "You didn't go to Spain with them?"

She licked the moisture of the drink from her lips and Win purposely turned his gaze away from her and onto the pile of burning logs. He had enough thoughts about kissing her without adding such tempting images to his mind.

She said, "At that time, I was still in college trying to finish out my teaching degree. Anyway, they were celebrating one of their anniversaries. They didn't need any of us kids along."

He turned his eyes back to her face. "So you have four siblings," he commented. "Are any of them teachers, like you?"

She chuckled as though the idea of her brothers or sister teaching school was definitely amusing. "No. They all think I'm a glutton for punishment to be a teacher. I mean, don't get me wrong, they admire the profession and they've always supported my desire to teach. But in their opinion, they could find plenty of jobs with less stress."

He chuckled wryly. "The way I see it, every job carries some sort of stress with it. What do your siblings do for a living?"

"Billy, the oldest, is a rancher and helps Dad take care

of the Bonnie B. He's married to Charlotte Taylor and she's currently pregnant. They also have three teenagers, Branson, Nicky and Jill. My other brothers, Theo and Jace, help work the family ranch, too. On the side, Theo does a podcast called *This Ranching Life* and Jace is a volunteer firefighter for the Bronco area. My sister, Robin, who's three years older than me, is married to Dylan Sanchez, and she has a horse therapeutics line that's doing well for her. They don't have any kids. Not yet, that is."

"What about Theo and Jace?" he asked. "Are they married?"

"Theo is engaged to Bethany McCreery. She's six months pregnant, so they'll soon be parents. And Jace is engaged to Tamara Hanson. She's a nurse and they have a fourteen-month-old son, Frankie."

She'd given him a load of information to digest and keep straight, but one thing stuck out clearly to Win. Each of Stacy's three brothers had families and a sister who was married, but with no children yet. So why was Stacy still single? True, she was only twenty-eight, which was still very young. But, to Win, she seemed like a woman who'd put a husband and children high on her lists of life goals. Just guessing, he'd bet she didn't even have a special boyfriend. Otherwise, when her car had failed to start earlier tonight, she would've called the guy for help.

Casually sipping his drink, he glanced at her from the corner of his eye. "Sounds like your siblings are busy expanding the Abernathy family. I'm surprised you're not yet married or engaged."

Her lips formed a smile, as though to imply his question hadn't bothered her, yet he could see a rosy-pink color staining her cheeks. He'd thought women had quit blushing long ago. Tara had certainly never expressed any kind of embarrassment with pink cheeks. He couldn't remember his late wife blushing, either. Yvette hadn't been a reserved type like Stacy. She'd been more of a rough-and-tumble girl who'd worked hard all of her life.

"If you're wondering if I have something against love or marriage, I don't," she said. "It's just that I...haven't met the right man yet."

"Particular, eh?"

"Not necessarily particular," she retorted. "I happen to think a person needs to be careful when they're choosing a lifelong mate. It's not like you're trying to decide if you want apple pie or cherry for dessert, you know."

His question had certainly ignited a spark in her and as his gaze slipped over her face, he decided he liked the way it made her blue eyes glimmer and her lips pucker into a perfect little bow. A very kissable bow, at that, he thought.

Forcing his eyes off her lips, he said, "Well, sometimes a person takes so long trying to decide which flavor he wants that the pie ends up spoiling. And that's a real waste."

A frown puckered the middle of her forehead. "What I consider a waste is devoting yourself to someone who, in the end, doesn't give a darn about your feelings."

The hard edge to her voice surprised him and he shifted around on the cushion to study her more closely. "Has that happened to you?"

She looked over at him and Win noticed a hollowness to her expression that implied she was carrying an empty spot inside her. Why? he wondered.

She sighed. "No. Not really. Oh, I've had a few relationships that fizzled, but I wasn't really that invested in any of them."

His lips twisted. "Did you ever think that might have been the reason they fizzled?"

"Sure. But you can't force yourself to feel something that isn't there. You know?"

Oh yes, he definitely knew how boring and tedious and even depressing it had been dating Tara. The woman had tried so hard to make him fall in love and propose marriage to her. But he'd not been interested in either of those things and the more she'd pushed and demanded, the more Win had withdrawn. He'd lost his one true soulmate. He wasn't looking to find another. Could it be that Stacy was a bit like Win and had given up on finding a lifelong partner?

He said, "Yeah. I'm an expert on losing interest."

Her brows rose slightly, but thankfully she didn't pursue his remark. Still, he couldn't help but wonder what she was thinking about him now. That he expected too much from a woman?

Telling himself her opinion didn't matter, he drained the last of his drink and was placing the empty glass on an end table next to his right elbow when a young man wearing faded jeans and flannel shirt, and a blond woman in a flowered maxi-dress strolled into the room. The man's arm was snugged affectionately around the woman's pregnant waist and the two were exchanging warm glances, making it obvious they were a couple.

"Mom told us we had company," the man said to Stacy as he glanced at Win. "We thought we'd come say hello."

"Hi, you two." Stacy immediately rose to her feet, gave the couple a brief hug, then gestured for Win to join them. "Meet Win Jackson. He's the new agribusiness teacher at Bronco High School. And, Win, this is my brother Billy and his wife, Charlotte."

Win stood and walked over to the young rancher and his wife. "A pleasure to meet you both," he said as he shook hands with Billy and then Charlotte.

"The pleasure is ours," Billy said. "It's always nice to have company. And we're especially glad Stacy had enough sense to invite you out to the Bonnie B for dinner."

Win noticed Stacy's cheeks once again turned pink. Obviously, it was making her feel awkward to have Billy linking the two of them together.

"Uh, I didn't exactly invite him," Stacy quickly corrected. "I had car trouble and Win was kind enough to bring me home."

"And your mother insisted I stay for dinner," Win added to her explanation.

"Sounds like Bonnie," Charlotte said with a wide smile. "Are those your sons we saw in the kitchen?"

Win nodded. "Joshua and Oliver. I hope they weren't trying to eat all of Bonnie's cookies."

Billy chuckled. "She'd never allow that. She's actually put them and our kids to work setting the table. We have three teenagers. Branson, Nicky and Jill."

"Seventeen, fifteen and fourteen," Charlotte told him. "Billy says they're the reason he's starting to gray at the temples."

Billy's grin was full of pride. "They're basically good kids. We love 'em lots, don't we, honey?"

"More than anything," she agreed then patted her rotund belly. "And we already love this little one, too."

Billy reached over and placed a hand on the growing child and Charlotte cast her husband a look that caused Win to remember back when his wife had once looked at him with deep, genuine love. But that part of his life was over and finished, he thought dully.

Stacy lightly cleared her throat. "Would you two like something to drink? We just had some of Mom's fizzy fruit juice."

Billy said, "Actually, I think dinner is just about ready. Dad just came in and has gone to wash up. And Robin and Dylan are supposed to be here any minute."

"Oh. They're coming tonight?" Stacy asked.

"That's what Bonnie told us," Charlotte said.

Hearing more people would be arriving caused Win to cast a concerned look at Stacy. "I'm thinking I should take the boys on home. Your mother has plenty of dinner guests without us causing more work for her."

Billy let out an easy laugh. "Forget it, Win. Most every night of the week, some of us are here to eat. If we didn't show up, Mom would think something was wrong. She's used to her kids popping in and out, so she always cooks plenty."

"That's right, Win," Charlotte added. "The more, the merrier. Bonnie could never have too many mouths to feed."

"Yes, but we're not family," he pointed out. "We're only here by happenstance."

"Listen, Win," Billy said, "you helped my sister. That makes you a friend of the family."

Family. Each time he heard the word, it was like a punch in the gut. He didn't need these reminders of all he'd lost—of everything his boys had lost when their mother died. But he couldn't just walk out. Stacy would view him as an ungrateful creep.

And why should that matter, Win? You didn't care what Tara thought when you walked out on her.

"Hey, Dad, Grandma says dinner is ready."

The announcement interrupted Win's dour thoughts and he glanced over to see a tall boy with dark blond hair wearing jeans and a graphic T-shirt. Obviously, he was one of Billy's sons.

"Thanks, Branson. We'll be right there," Billy told him.

The teenager quickly disappeared and the four adults slowly migrated from the room. Out in the hallway, Stacy once again walked close to Win's side and he was surprised at how nice and natural it felt to have her next to him.

As the group moved down the hallway, Stacy said, "Billy, you might be interested to know that Win has a ranch not far from here—the J Barb."

"So that place belongs to you now," Billy stated. "I'd heard someone had purchased the property, but I didn't know who. It used to be a profitable ranch at one time, but when the owner got too old to take care of things, it began to get run down. He had a couple of kids, but they never cared to help him."

"His children were the ones who sold the property," Win replied. "I got the impression they wanted to get it off their hands."

"Yeah, so much for leaving your kids a legacy," Billy said somewhat sorrowfully.

"Not everyone has a desire to be a rancher," Stacy told her brother.

Billy laughed. "You would say that."

When they reached the dining room, Stacy quickly introduced Win to her father, Asa, a vibrant man with a strong handshake and an affable smile. Her sister Robin and husband, Dylan Sanchez, had also arrived and they greeted Win as though it wasn't unusual to have extra company at the Abernathy dinner table.

Once everyone was seated and the bowls of food began to make their way around the table, Asa asked, "So, what do you think of Bronco, Win?"

"So far, I'm glad I made the move," Win replied. He ladled a serving of macaroni and cheese onto his plate then handed the bowl to Stacy, who was seated next to him. "The town is a lot tighter knit than I thought it would be."

Bonnie laughed. "You have to be careful what you say and who you say it to, Win. Otherwise, you might offend someone's friend or relative."

"I'm definitely learning to watch what I say around Bronco," Win told her.

Oliver spoke up. "Dad says gossiping about people is mean, so I don't gossip about anyone."

Joshua grunted and rolled his eyes, causing Billy's three teenagers to snicker with amusement. At the same time, Win noticed Stacy smiling with approval at Oliver. It was no wonder his young son viewed her as an angel, he thought. She seemed to want to shield him from the banter of his older brother.

"I think that's very admirable of you, Oliver," she said. "If everyone made an effort not to gossip, we'd all be better off."

"True," Robin agreed then added jokingly, "but what would that leave us to talk about? The weather?"

"I've heard enough about the weather." Charlotte spoke up. "I want to know if anyone has heard any news about Winona."

Stacy glanced over at Win. "Have you ever met Winona Cobbs?"

"No. I can't say that I've heard that name," Win told her. "Is she a relative?"

Asa cleared his throat and Billy chuckled under his breath.

Win glanced around the table while wondering if his innocent question had opened a can of worms.

"Uh, when she was very young, she had a romance with an Abernathy ancestor that produced a child," Stacy explained. "It's a very long story. But to simplify things, that child made Winona connected to the Abernathys, but she isn't actually related to the family. Anyway, she's ninety-seven years old now, and she's gone missing."

"She's also Bronco's resident psychic," Billy added. "Don't forget that part."

"Plus, she's engaged to be married to Dylan's uncle, Stanley Sanchez," Robin said. "He's a young eighty-seven."

Win frowned with bewilderment. "I want to make sure I'm getting this straight. A ninety-seven-year-old psychic, who's engaged to be married to a man ten years her junior, has gone missing?"

"I realize this all probably sounds strange to you, Win," Bonnie said, "but if you knew Winona, you'd understand. You'd never guess she's in her nineties. And she actually is a psychic. Many of her premonitions have come true."

Robin cast her husband a look of concern. "Tell Win the rest of the story."

"There isn't a whole lot to tell," Dylan said with a helpless shrug. "When Uncle Stanley first met Winona, it was love at first sight for him and she seemed madly in love with him. Two years ago, they got engaged and he put a beautiful amethyst ring on her finger."

"Which she proudly showed off to everyone." Robin emphasized. "And their wedding was going to be a big romantic affair."

Nodding, Dylan said, "Which was going to take place a few weeks ago. But the day of the wedding, Winona just suddenly vanished without a trace. Everyone searched, but she couldn't be found, and a lot of folks around town believe she simply ran off because she got cold feet."

Win glanced around the table. "I'm assuming you folks don't believe that's the case."

"No!" Robin exclaimed while Dylan shook his head. "We don't know what to believe! All of us who are close to Winona think she might have been kidnapped. Stanley is convinced that something bad has happened to her. But then, her daughter Daisy received a note from Winona stating everything was well with her and she left because she needed to be free. Winona ended by apologizing for leaving without a word, but she thought it would be easier that way—without painful goodbyes."

Win frowned. "Just when I thought this story about Winona couldn't get any stranger, it does," he remarked and glanced questioningly at Dylan. "Did the letter look as though Winona actually wrote it?"

Dylan answered. "Well, at ninety-seven, her handwriting is a bit shaky, but Uncle Stanley believes she wrote it."

"What does your uncle think about her explanation?" Win asked.

"Stanley doesn't believe a word of it," Dylan told him. "And as you might guess, he's totally despondent. He can't believe that Winona jilted him. He's afraid that something bad must have happened to her, otherwise, he believes she would come back to him. This ordeal has been especially hard on Uncle Stanley because his beloved wife died about a year before he moved to Bronco in 2022. So he hadn't been a widower for very long when he met and fell in love with Winona."

"I'm sorry your uncle is going through this. Losing a loved one…isn't easy." As soon as Win said the words, everyone except Joshua and Oliver looked curiously at him and he realized the Abernathys were all waiting for an explanation. "I'm a widower. That's, uh, how I can relate to Stanley's sorrow."

Bonnie cast him an empathetic look. "Oh. We didn't know, Win. But we're glad you told us."

A moment of awkward silence passed and Win was wondering how he'd ever gotten into this uncomfortable situation in the first place, when he suddenly felt Stacy's hand give his knee a comforting pat. The notion that she seemed to understand how he was feeling touched him in a way he would've never expected.

"Sometimes people ask me if I have a mom and I tell them no. 'Cause, I don't," Oliver said glumly.

Even though the rib roast he'd been eating was delicious, Win felt a little sick at the lost look on his son's face. It was one thing to have Oliver lamenting to Win in private over the fact that he was motherless, but hearing him say it in front of a group of people he'd only just met was a whole other matter.

Billy's daughter Jill glanced down the table at Oliver and gave him an encouraging smile. "But you might get another mother, Oliver. Me and my brothers did and she's super!"

Another mother. Apparently, Charlotte wasn't the biological mother to these three teenagers, but from the glowing expression on the woman's face, he could see none of that mattered. She considered them her children, too. Win had to wonder if Billy realized how very lucky he was to have a whole family.

"Thank you, Jill. That's a super nice compliment," Charlotte told her.

"Well, I'm just fine without a mom," Joshua retorted.

Joshua's sulky tone didn't surprise Win, but he was a bit stunned that his son had spouted such a thing in front of the Abernathys. But he supposed Joshua didn't want these kids, who were his own age, thinking he was hurting and vulnerable. Putting on a cool and tough front seemed especially important to him now.

"Gosh, I wouldn't want to be without mine," Branson remarked.

Joshua's expression turned sheepish and he quickly turned his attention to the food on his plate. After that, the conversation around the table moved on to other things. Asa and Billy both wanted to hear about the J Barb and Bonnie talked about the Bronco Harvest Festival, an event that took place every October at the Bronco Fairgrounds. The mere mention of carnival rides and a midway got the kids all excited and Billy's teenagers eagerly explained to Joshua and Oliver what the festival usually entailed. Then Asa was quick to remind everyone that the festival wouldn't be the only big event to be held next month in Bronco. The Golden Buckle Rodeo was going to be taking place at the Bronco Convention Center and, supposedly, Brooks Langtree, the first Black rodeo rider to be awarded the Golden Buckle thirty years ago, was returning to Bronco for the big celebration.

Win was glad his sons had been given something fun to think about and he was especially glad to see them making friends with Billy's three kids. But as for him, he'd definitely had more than enough family unity for one night. He simply wanted to go home and forget about the soft, pretty blonde sitting next to him. He wanted to forget the pleasure he'd felt when she'd given his knee an encouraging pat and the smiles she'd slanted him throughout the meal. Oh yes, he had to forget all those things, or he was going to be in a far worse mess than he'd found himself in with marriage-minded Tara.

Yet, to be fair, Stacy wasn't anything like Tara. Not in looks or personality. The tall brunette had been overly outgoing with a taste for the flamboyant. She'd also been the take-charge kind, who'd go to great lengths to get whatever she wanted. In the beginning, she'd been a fun date and just what Win had needed at the time to get his mind off losing the most important person in his life. Unfortunately, Tara had viewed every date as one step closer to the marriage altar. When he'd finally made it clear he wasn't interested in matrimony, she'd unsheathed her claws and proceeded to do a hatchet job on his reputation. And because she'd worked as a receptionist at the same school in Whitehorn where he'd taught agribusiness, she'd made his life and his job so miserable he'd sold his home and moved to Bronco to escape.

No. Even if a man broke Stacy's heart, he couldn't see her being vengeful. Frankly, Win couldn't even picture her being romantically interested in him. She was particular. She'd said so herself. She was probably looking to start a life with a young man with a clean slate. Not one who was twelve years older than she, plus a widower with two boys to raise.

Still, each time he glanced at her lovely face, he could easily picture himself falling for her in a head-over-heels kind of way. And where his heart was concerned, that made her a dangerous woman.

Chapter Four

Throughout the meal, there had been moments when Stacy had sensed Win was uncomfortable dealing with her big family. But there had also been occasions when she'd caught him looking at her with something like interest in his eyes. She was hardly an expert on men, but she had to believe he found her attractive. She just didn't know if the attraction would ever be deep enough to draw him to her.

By the time everyone had finished eating the main meal, Stacy half expected Win to forgo coffee and dessert and quickly say his goodbyes. But he surprised her by staying for the cherry cobbler and even waiting until Joshua and Oliver finished a second helping before he announced they had to be heading home.

Stacy followed them out to the foyer where the boys retrieved their jackets from the hall tree. While they pulled on the garments, Stacy reached for a plaid shawl her mother kept hanging by the door.

"I'll walk you out," she said to Win.

He glanced at her. "That isn't necessary. But it's nice of you."

Smiling faintly, she draped the knit fabric around her shoulders. "You're my guests. Of course, I want to see you off."

Outside, the boys trotted off the porch and on to the truck, leaving Stacy and Win to follow at their own pace. As they walked, she wondered how it would feel to be on a date with this man and have him reach for hand. How would it feel to have his strong fingers wrapped tightly around hers?

The fantasy was pointless, she thought. Win wasn't her boyfriend and this evening was anything but a date. Still, having his company, even as a friend, had been very special to her. And she couldn't stop herself from having a spark of hope that something deeper might develop between them.

"I'm afraid my dead battery has wrecked your evening," she said. "But you did get a fairly good meal out of the deal."

"The meal was delicious, Stacy. I've not eaten so much in ages."

At least her mother's cooking had impressed him, Stacy thought, even if she hadn't. "I'm glad you enjoyed the food," she told him.

Side by side, they started down the steps and once again Stacy's mind began to wander. There were plenty of shadows along the walk to the truck. How would it feel to have him draw her into the darkness and kiss her? She'd kissed men before, but she had a feeling that the experience would be totally different with Win.

And what if he did kiss you, Stacy? You think a kiss from a man like Win would mean anything? He's not looking for a woman. Not on a permanent basis.

Shutting her mind against the scoffing voice in her head, she said, "The night is beautiful. Fall is my favorite time of the year. Lots of pumpkin treats, hot chocolate and roasting marshmallows. And the weather is perfect. Not too hot or cold."

"It's also a busy time with a new school year starting. But I do enjoy the mild weather."

She looked up at his profile etched against the glow of a yard lamp. "I imagine spring is probably your favorite time of the year."

"Hmm. Why would you think so?"

She laughed softly. "Because you're a rancher like my father and brothers. They're always happiest when they see green grass sprouting and knowing the days of spreading hay will soon be over."

He chuckled. "Smart deduction. Spring is a good time for ranchers. Green pastures and baby calves. Ranchers view those things as profit."

"Yes. Most every vocation boils down to money. But I have a feeling you're like my family—you don't just ranch to make money. You do it because you love the job."

He nodded. "Yeah. Like teaching."

"I was going to ask you earlier before dinner, but I didn't get a chance," she said. "What did you think about the school meeting tonight?"

"I had to keep pinching myself to stay awake," he admitted with a wry chuckle. "What about you?"

Instead of pinching herself, she'd been staring across the conference room at him and the few times she'd seen him staring back at her had given her the impression he might be interested enough to speak to her after the meeting. She'd been disappointed when he'd made a beeline for the door without even glancing her way. She'd even scolded herself for wasting such thoughts on the man.

"I hate to admit it, but most of the district meetings are pretty stale. At the elementary school, we teachers kind of get together on our own and try to come up with new and innovative ideas to keep the students interested in learning." She eyed him. "I have an idea that it's much easier keeping seven-year-olds involved in their lessons than it is teenagers. I imagine they try your patience."

His grunt was full of amusement. "You know how a rubber band grows thin just before it snaps? Well, there are times that my patience stretches that thin. But, on a whole, I enjoy the kids."

"So do I," she murmured. "I can't imagine being anything else but a teacher."

"What about being a mother?"

The unexpected question very nearly caused her to stumble and his hand slipped under her elbow to steady her balance as they covered the last few feet to the truck.

"I'm hoping the children will come," she told him. "Whenever I find the right man."

"Ah, yes, the one who can hold your interest."

He was teasing and she was glad. It was far, far too early for Win to learn just how quickly she was becoming infatuated with him. And keeping things light between them for now was probably for the best. Still, she couldn't help thinking how one little innocent kiss from him would've made her whole week.

The foolish thought made her silently groan. She wasn't being herself tonight, she thought. It wasn't like her to lose her head over a good looking man. Especially one who didn't appear to be the least bit interested in her.

Shoving that thought aside, she forced out a soft laugh. "He'll come along. Sooner or later."

They reached the driver's door of the truck and he caught her completely by surprise by reaching out and enveloping her hand between both of his. His palm was a bit rough and callused, and the warmth of his skin pressed against hers sent a streak of sizzling heat all the way up her arm.

"Thank you for the dinner, Stacy."

A blush was burning her cheeks, but with any luck, her face was partially hidden from him by the shadows. She drew in a long breath then slowly eased it past her lips. "You already thanked Mom, and she's the one who deserves your appreciation. Not me."

He continued to hold her hand and Stacy desperately wished she knew what he was actually thinking. Throughout this whole evening, he'd been giving her all kinds of mixed signals. At times, she'd gotten the impression he'd wanted to jump to his feet and run for his life. But now, as they stood close together in the semi-darkness, she was getting the odd feeling that he was reluctant to say goodbye.

"It was gracious of your family to have us. And it was good for Joshua and Oliver to have a sit-down dinner with someone other than their father."

What about him? Stacy wanted to ask. Had any part of the evening been good for him? More importantly, was there a chance she'd ever spend time with him again?

Deciding she didn't know him well enough to voice her questions out loud, she merely said, "I'm glad you think so."

He dropped her hand and opened the truck door. Stacy used the moment to stick her head inside the cab to tell Joshua and Oliver good night.

"You have to come eat with us next time," Oliver told her.

"Thank you for the invitation, Oliver. I'll think about it."

She moved aside and Win climbed into the driver's seat.

"Good night, Stacy," he said. "Maybe we'll run into each other again sometime."

Only by happenstance, she thought dully. Because he obviously wasn't going to repeat Oliver's invitation or ask her for her phone number. "Well, you and the boys should stop by the ranch again. We all enjoyed your company."

He started the engine. "Nice of you to offer, Stacy. But I rarely have time for much of anything except school and taking care of things at home."

No time for dating? She was still wondering about Tara back in Whitehorn. Oliver had implied they'd moved from there to get away from the woman. Had she been Win's steady girlfriend? A mistress, who'd grown too clingy? Stacy was shocked at just how much she wanted to learn about Win's life.

"Well, just so you know you're welcome," she said.

He nodded then shut the door, ending any opportunity for her to say more, and as the truck pulled away, Stacy lifted a hand in farewell.

Win Jackson was an enigma, she thought as she watched the taillights of the truck fade into the distance. If she had any sense, she'd put him on her *don't bother* list. But where men were concerned, she'd spent the past few years playing it safe. Maybe that made her a coward, but she'd not always been so cautious. No, as a teenager, she'd done her fair share of dating and in spite of the normal drama associated with boys of that age, she'd survived without a broken heart.

By the time she'd entered college she'd thought she was ready for a serious relationship and when she'd met Spence she'd believed he was truly her dream man. Good looking, smart and ambitious, he'd checked all the right boxes on her list. They'd dated steadily for nearly a year and he'd begun talking about the two of them having a future to-gether. He'd even visited the Bonnie B to meet her parents. But then suddenly, without any warning, he'd called it quits and started dating someone else. His desertion had been humiliating and heartbreaking. And had left her leery to trust her happiness to any man.

Nearly eight years had passed since then and though Stacy had gotten over losing Spense long ago, she'd not forgotten the hard lesson learned about trusting her heart to someone. Yet something about Win made her want to throw caution to the wind. He made her wonder if the time had come for her to take a few risks. Suffering through a broken heart couldn't be any worse than being alone and wondering when, or if, the right man would ever come along.

The following Saturday dawned clear and just warm enough to not have to deal with a jacket. It was the sort of day Win loved to use working around the ranch. Especially doing some needed repairs to a cross fence, along with exercising the horses. Instead, he and his sons were headed to the annual back-to-school picnic being held at Bronco City Park.

Actually, it wasn't mandatory that all teachers attend the social function, but because Win was new to Bronco High School, he felt it was important for the parents and students to see him making an effort to be a part of the community and the school.

"Dad, do you think we'll see Ms. Abernathy at the picnic?" Oliver asked as Win searched for a spot to park the truck.

"I don't know, son. We might."

"Why do you care if she's at the picnic?" Joshua asked with a heavy dose of sarcasm. "She's just a teacher. That's all. And you see plenty of teachers at school."

"Stacy is more than a teacher," Oliver shot back at his brother. "She's my friend, too. And I like her a whole lot. So does Dad."

Even though Win was concentrating on spotting an empty parking space, he didn't miss his sons' conversation. Nothing much had changed since the night they'd had dinner with the Abernathys. Oliver was still infatuated with Stacy, while Joshua wanted to cut her and all women down whenever he was given the opportunity.

"Do you, Dad?"

Joshua's question was more like a challenge than a desire to know the truth, and Win had to bite back a weary sigh. Once they'd gotten home from the Abernathys' the other night, Win had taken his elder son aside and talked to him about the snide remarks he'd made about not needing a mother. Even though it had been seven years since Yvette had died, Win realized Joshua still missed her terribly. He also understood that, at fifteen, Joshua was trying to appear cool and indifferent. But Joshua needed to learn the difference between being cool and being rude.

"Yes, I like Stacy. She's a very nice woman," Win answered his question.

"Does that mean we can go back to the Bonnie B real soon?" Oliver asked eagerly.

Win stifled a groan. Three days had passed since he and his sons had sat at the Abernathy dinner table, and the time had done little to get Stacy out of his mind. Frankly, he didn't understand why he was having these obsessive thoughts about her. It wasn't like she was a dazzling beauty, or a provocative siren attempting to seduce him. She was simply kind and pretty and sweet.

"We haven't been invited," he told Oliver.

He braked the truck to a halt in the nearest parking slot he could find, which was more than a block away from the park. Apparently, the picnic was a big deal for the Bronco folks, he mused.

Oliver was quick to correct Win. "We sure have been invited," he said. "Stacy said for us to come visit anytime. Remember?"

"Yes, I do," Win replied.

He also remembered vividly how it had felt to hold her soft little hand and watch shadows flicker furtively across her lovely face. The thought of bending his head and kissing her had burned in his brain. But knowing his sons had been sitting in the back seat of the truck had put a damper on the urge. That had probably been for the best, because something told him that one kiss from her wouldn't have been enough.

They made the short walk to the park in less than two minutes and as they merged onto a grassy area near the picnic tables, where a crowd of people had already gathered for the back-to-school event. Children were running and playing, and excited shrieks and happy laughter filled the air. Because it was still a little early for lunch, he didn't see anyone eating yet, but some folks had already taken seats at the picnic tables and spread blankets on the ground.

"Gosh, this place is running over with people!" Joshua exclaimed as they worked their way into the edge of the crowd. "Do you see anybody you know, Dad?"

Joshua had barely gotten the question out when Win spotted Anthony, along with a history teacher who doubled as an assistant baseball coach.

"Yes, I do. There's Anthony and Raymond. Let's go say hello."

Win talked to his colleagues for a few minutes before he noticed Joshua and Oliver practically jumping up and down to move on and hunt for their friends.

Once they left the two coaches and headed deeper into the crowd, Joshua found a group of his high school friends and, a short distance away, Oliver ran into his best buddy, Artie, who'd brought his collie dog to the picnic. Win was content to stand in the shade of an evergreen tree and watch the youngsters keep the dog busy fetching a Frisbee.

"Hello, Win."

The soft familiar voice caused his pulse to quicken and he couldn't stop himself from smiling as he turned to see Stacy striding up to him. Wearing a pair of dark blue jeans and a black cotton sweater with long sleeves, she had pulled her hair up into a wavy ponytail and gold hoops dangled from her ears. She looked incredibly sexy and very different from the prim teacher attending the district meeting.

"Hello, Stacy. Nice to see you."

She smiled back at him. "I wondered if you'd come today."

He chuckled. "You sound as though you expected me to skip this picnic."

She laughed. "You don't exactly seem like the picnic type. More like the chuckwagon-and-eating-around-the-campfire kind of guy."

"Yeah, with a herd of bawling cattle in the background," he added with a wry grin. "To be honest, that's the best kind of outdoor eating. But I don't have much opportunity to do it. Did you come to the picnic alone?"

She nodded. "Yes. But I've already run into several colleagues and friends."

"Am I included in the friends group?" he asked.

The impish smile on her lips was enough to lift his spirits.

"Of course, you're included," she said then darted a quick glance around her. "Where are the boys?"

He gestured to a spot beyond his right shoulder where a group of young people had gathered around a picnic table.

"Joshua is over there with his friends. And Oliver is on the playground with Artie and his dog."

She glanced over to her right just in time to see Oliver toss the Frisbee. The dog jumped and caught the piece of plastic long before it hit the ground and both boys shouted in triumph.

"Looks like those two are having a blast," she said.

"Artie is Oliver's best friend, so I'm glad he's here and the two can spend some time together away from school."

"I taught Artie when he was in second grade. He's a good kid. At that time, his mother was concerned about the boy's learning skills, but he turned out to be an A student."

"Hmm. Sometimes parents expect too much from their kids. Or maybe I should say, demand too much. I often have to remind myself that my sons aren't adults and I can't expect them to behave as such."

She nodded. "I think all adults are guilty of expecting too much from children. Including me. I just hope that whenever I have children of my own I won't treat them as little students. I want to believe I'll forget I'm a teacher and discipline them as a loving mother with a firm hand."

He scanned the soft expression on her face. "You'd like to have children?"

"Ever since I was a young girl I've dreamed about having a house full of children." She glanced at him and shrugged. "Obviously I've not started on a family yet. But I hope to— as soon as I find the right man."

As Win watched a wan smile tilt her lips, he found himself thinking she would eventually make a great mother for some man's children. He imagined she'd be loving but firm when necessary. Most of all, she would put her children's happiness and well-being before her own. Yes, she'd be very maternal and nurturing, he imagined. And a woman

like her deserved to have a family of her own. But the idea
of her getting that close to some other man bothered him
in a way that he never expected.

"What kind of man would be right for you?" he asked.

"Well, I want him to be honest and trustworthy. Com-
passionate toward others, but strong enough to stand up for
himself and his beliefs. He'd need to be a man who loves
children and wants plenty of his own. And, of course, I
want him to love me, just for being me. See, my ideal man
is nothing out of the ordinary," she said with a wide smile.

"Sounds good. But you left out a major detail. You want
to be in love with him, don't you?"

Pink color seeped into her cheeks before her gaze darted
away from his. "Absolutely. Loving him would be my first
requirement."

He shook his head as he tried to shake away the image
of her wrapped in a passionate embrace with a man she'd
vowed to love until death parted them.

She cleared her throat. "Now back to being a parent, from
what I see, you do a great job with your sons."

"I, uh, don't know about great. I try. I feel like I should
apologize to you and your family for Joshua's rude remarks
at the dinner table the other night. I'm sure Billy's kids
thought he sounded like a creep."

"I'm pretty sure they understand that Joshua is still hurting because he lost his mother."

He sighed. "I hope so. I had a talk with him once we
got home that night. Whether it will make a difference is
anybody's guess."

Her expression was full of empathy as she looked at him.
"It can't have been easy raising your sons alone after your
wife died. But you must be very glad that you have them."

She seemed to understand his situation far better than

Tara ever had. Moreover, Stacy didn't resent the fact that he had two sons; she actually cared about their welfare.

Watch it, Win. Right now, all you're seeing in Stacy is her good qualities. She's still a woman. Especially a woman who's the marrying kind. Just what you don't want.

Shutting out the mocking voice, he said, "You're right. I'm very blessed to have my boys."

"Tell me about your wife. Was she a strict mother?"

Not many people asked him about Yvette. Probably because they thought bringing up her memory would upset him. But Stacy's question didn't bother him. In fact, it felt good not to have to skirt around the subject of his late wife.

"Yvette was actually stricter with the boys than I've ever been. She wanted them to grow up strong. Both morally and physically and though they were very young when she died, I think she'd managed to start them out in life on a solid foundation."

"Did the four of you do many family things together?"

He looked out across the grassy slope of lawn as memories of his life with Yvette paraded through the back of his mind. "As much as we could. We were like most couples. Busy with our jobs and we had the ranch to care for. But we did take the boys to family type events and always a camping trip in the summer."

She let out a soft sigh. "I'm sure you miss her. And I'm sorry you lost her. Sometimes life is very unfair."

Win could see she truly was sorry about Yvette's passing and the fact drew him to her in a way he'd never expected.

After a stretch of silence passed between them, she cleared her throat and spoke. "I see some of my colleagues have gathered at the picnic table near the cottonwood tree. Would you like to walk over and meet them?"

"Sure," he said. "Just let me tell Oliver where I'll be in case he starts looking for me."

She nodded. "I'll come with you and say hello."

They talked to Oliver a moment then left him playing with Artie and the dog.

"I understand this back-to-school picnic happens every year," Win said as the two of them walked together across a grassy slope. "Do you attend every year?"

"Always. This event has been going on for as long as I can remember. I think the kids would be in an uproar if we didn't have it."

She smelled like sunshine and wind and something else that was sweet and soft. The scent was evocative, almost as much as the feel of her hand resting gently on his forearm. Why hadn't he noticed these things about other women? he wondered. What was it about Stacy that made him think about such feminine nuances? He didn't know. He only knew that when he was with her, he felt more alive than he had in years.

Once they reached the table near the cottonwood, Stacy introduced Win to Emma Garner and Reginald Porter, along with Carrie Waters and Amelia Holsten.

"Emma teaches first grade, Reggie teaches fourth, Carrie is an aide and Amelia handles the kindergarten class," she explained to Win.

"Nice to meet all of you," Win said as he shook hands with each one. "And good to see you again, Reggie. I hope Oliver hasn't been giving you a bad time so far."

Stacy laughed with embarrassment. "What was I thinking? I forgot that Reggie was Oliver's teacher, so you two have obviously already met."

The middle-aged man with thinning hair and droopy

features smiled and shook his head. "Oliver is polite and very attentive. I only wish I had more students like him."

"I'm relieved to hear it," Win told Reggie.

"Oh, here comes Dante and Eloise and little Merry," Emma announced. "Dante teaches third grade at Bronco Elementary."

Win turned to see a couple, both with dark brown hair and in their early thirties. The man was holding a little girl that Win would guess to be somewhere around a year old. Presently, the baby was squirming and wriggling in an effort to stand on the ground.

"Merry sees the girls on the playground across the way playing soccer and thinks she's big enough to join them," Eloise said with indulgent smile for the toddler.

"She'll be their age before you know it," Stacy told her. Then placing a hand on Win's arm, she quickly introduced him to the married couple, while adding, "Dante and Eloise are newlyweds. They had a lovely little backyard ceremony a few weeks ago."

"Congratulations," Win told the beaming couple.

"Thanks," Dante told him. "We were going to have a big wedding but with all the trauma going on with Uncle Stanley and Winona's disappearance we thought it best to keep everything low-key."

"Yes, Stacy has told me about the situation with your uncle and Winona. I hope everything turns out well."

"Thanks for your concern," Dante told him.

"Dylan, whom you met during dinner at the Bonnie B is Dante's brother," Stacy told Win.

"I see the resemblance," Win told him, adding with a chuckle, "I also see why the Abernathys warned me about saying anything about anyone around town, unless you're saying something nice, that is. Everyone seems to be related or best friends."

Dante laughed. "The rule of living in a town like Bronco," he said. "So, you're the new agribusiness teacher I've been hearing about. Welcome."

"Thanks," Win replied. "I hope what you've been hearing isn't too bad."

"On the contrary. Everyone who's mentioned you has great things to say. This area of the state thrives on agriculture, so we need teachers like you to educate the next generation of ranchers and farmers."

"Are you a rancher, along with being a teacher?" Win asked him.

"Dante helps his brother Dylan run a car dealership," Eloise answered for her husband. "You wouldn't happen to be looking to purchase a new vehicle, would you?"

Everyone laughed at Eloise's playful sales pitch and, for the next few minutes, the group talked about everything from school events to the latest local news.

Eventually, Oliver arrived to inform his father he was getting hungry, and a quick glance at his watch told Win he'd already been at the park much longer than he'd planned.

"Okay, son," he told Oliver. "We'll go find Joshua."

He'd said his goodbyes to the group and was walking away with Oliver at his side when Stacy quickly caught up with them.

"I don't mean to pry, Win, but did you bring lunch for you and the boys?"

He paused to answer her. "No. I had several chores to take care of at the ranch before we left the J Barb to come here. I didn't really have time to make anything, so I promised the kids I'd let them eat takeout."

"Oh. Well, fast food is fun, but you'd have to leave the

park to eat." She encompassed Win and Oliver with an eager smile. "I brought a picnic basket with enough food for several people. I'd love to share it with you three. That is, if you like fried chicken and a few other things to go with it."

Oliver began to jump excitedly on his toes. "Fried chicken! Mmm! Can we eat with Ms. Abernathy, Dad? I love fried chicken!"

Win looked at her. Had she extended the invitation because she felt sorry for him and wanted to be polite? Or did she really want his company? He hoped it was the latter but then promptly wondered about his own motives. Why did he want to spend time with this woman when he knew there could never be anything serious between them?

He didn't want serious. He didn't want a relationship where he might risk opening his heart and having it crushed all over again. He couldn't live through that again, he thought bleakly. And yet, something about Stacy made him want to be close to her. To pretend, just for a little while, that he could have a whole family again. Maybe that made him a fool. Or maybe he was finally finding the courage he'd lost seven years ago.

"It sounds delicious. But we'd be imposing on you," Win told her. "Especially after we've already had one Abernathy dinner."

She laughed lightly. "I promise you, Win, two or even three Abernathy dinners wouldn't be an imposition. And I'd hate to eat alone."

Oliver said, "Yeah, Dad, it would be sad if Ms. Abernathy had to eat at a picnic all by herself."

"You are so right, Oliver." Smiling, she gave the boy's shoulders an affectionate squeeze then glanced hopefully at Win. "My basket is in my car. It's parked not far from here."

Win couldn't stop a smile from spreading across his face

any more than he could dampen the joy he was suddenly feeling. "Okay. There's no way I can refuse your offer. Oliver would never forgive me. And I'm getting fairly hungry myself."

"Great," she said. "I'll let you guys do all the toting."

"It's the least we can do," Win told her.

The three of them started walking to the far side of the park where her car was located and, along the way, Win reached for her hand. She didn't hesitate to wrap her fingers around his.

The sweet connection caused his chest to swell with an emotion he couldn't quite describe. He only knew that the feeling was nice and warm and he wasn't sure he wanted it to go away.

Chapter Five

Earlier this morning, while Stacy had been getting ready to drive into town for the picnic, she'd wondered if Win would be taking part in the school event. It wasn't mandatory for teachers to attend the picnic and she figured he'd much rather use his Saturday to work on his ranch. Still, she'd hoped he might feel obligated to take his sons and she could accidentally-on-purpose run into him.

She'd been chatting with Emma and Carrie when she'd spotted him standing in the shade of the cottonwood. Dressed all in denim with his black hat and cowboy boots, he'd stood out from the crowd and his tall, sexy image had sent her pulse pounding. And now that he and his sons were sitting with her on a blanket spread on a patch of grassy ground, eating the lunch she'd provided, she felt sure the sky had grown bluer and the sun a bit brighter.

"Joshua, you could have invited your friend to join us," Stacy told the teenager. "We have plenty of food for her, too."

"That's okay, Ms. Abernathy. Katrina had already told me she'd have to eat with her parents and little sister Gena."

A few minutes ago, when the three of them had returned with the picnic basket and located Joshua, he'd been sitting beneath a tree with a young, dark-haired girl who appeared to be around his age. He'd introduced her as Katrina Wymore and she'd informed them that she and her family had only moved to Bronco a year ago. Stacy hadn't missed the furtive looks Joshua had been sending the girl and the shy smiles she'd been giving him.

"Gena is my age," Oliver interjected as he dug a chicken leg from a plastic container sitting in the middle of the blanket. "She sits at a desk next to me."

"Is she cute?" Win asked him then winked conspiringly at Stacy.

Oliver wrinkled his nose as he thoughtfully considered his father's question. "Yeah. I guess so. She has brown hair and freckles."

"Nothing wrong with freckles," Win told him. "You have a few of your own."

Oliver squinched up his nose even tighter. "No. But she talks. A whole lot."

Win chuckled. "Kind of like someone else I know. I feel sorry for Mr. Porter. He probably has to constantly quiet you two down."

Oliver cleared his mouth of chicken before he spoke. "We don't talk in class, Dad. We don't want to get in trouble."

Joshua released a scoffing grunt while Stacy and Win exchanged amused looks.

"Katrina says Gena never shuts up," Joshua said. "And I told her that Oliver was the same way."

"Why don't you shut up, Joshua?" Oliver snapped at his brother. "All you ever say is something mean."

Stacy hadn't been around Win's sons all that much, but enough to notice that if one boy fired off a cutting remark, the other one was quick to utter a sharp response. But in this case, Joshua wasn't shooting a string of sarcastic words back at his brother. Instead, he was studying Oliver in a bewildered way.

"Dad, do I always sound mean to Oliver?"

"Most generally," Win told his elder son.

Joshua's expression turned sheepish and Stacy wondered what was coming over the teenager. Win had told her that he'd had a talk with Joshua the other night. Perhaps some of what he'd said to the boy had sunk in.

"Gosh. I don't want to sound like a creep all the time," Joshua admitted in a plaintive voice.

The plastic fork in Oliver's hand hovered over the food on his plate as he looked at his brother. "It's okay, Joshua. I still like you anyway. You're my brother."

Grinning now, Joshua reached over and gave the top of Oliver's head a playful scruff.

"Yeah. You're a pretty good one, too."

Seemingly at peace, the boys went back to eating and, as Stacy watched them devouring the chicken, potato salad and baked beans, she thought how blessed Win was to have two sons. When he'd asked her if she wanted children, she'd not been able to express to him just how much she yearned to have babies and a family of her own. Each year that passed without so much as a special boyfriend in her life, the more she wondered if having a family wasn't meant for her. And the more she feared that the ideal man she'd described to Win would never walk into her life.

As for Win, it was tragic that he'd lost his wife, but Yvette lived on through Joshua and Oliver. He had to be thankful for his children, she thought. But did their constant presence make it impossible for Win to put his late wife behind him? She wanted to ask him. But she didn't want him to think she was prying into his private life.

"Did you cook all this food?" Win asked as he ladled more beans onto his paper plate. "It's delicious."

She cast him a guilty little smile. "Only the beans and dessert. I love to cook, but to tell you the truth, my teaching job doesn't leave me much extra time to do the things I enjoy. Thankfully, Mom took pity on me and made the chicken and potato salad when she saw I was so short on time."

He nodded with understanding. "Same with me. In fact, this morning I was thinking about how many things I needed to do on the ranch. But that's the way it is when you have a weekday job and another on the side."

"You must really like ranching because I imagine it, along with your teaching position, surely has you stretched."

A half grin quirked one corner of his lips. "I'm not complaining. I do love ranching and I want the boys to grow up learning about the vocation, even if they eventually decide to do something else with their lives. It's a good foundation. You know, going out in subzero temperatures and spreading hay or cleaning horse stalls. That kind of work has a way of keeping a person grounded."

She smiled. "Literally."

"So do you have something other than teaching that keeps you busy?" he asked.

Shrugging, she said, "I used to do all kinds of volunteer work for the library and getting hot meals to the elderly, but that was before teaching second grade took over my life. Now, the only extra work I do is to stay late at school on certain evenings to tutor adults who are trying to obtain their GEDs."

"That's an admirable job."

"I like to help people learn," Stacy said. "Especially when I know it's going to improve the quality of their life."

He nodded. "That's the same reason that keeps me in the

classroom. This might sound corny, but I like to think I'm helping give young people a better start on their future."

"If that's corny, then we're both old hat," she told him then cast him a curious glance. "You mentioned having a brother. What sort of job does he have?"

"Shawn is thirty-eight. Two years younger than me. He helps our dad run the family ranch near Whitehorn. Being a rancher is all he's ever wanted to do."

"Hmm. So, as far as ranching goes, you two are alike," she commented. "Is he married?"

"He was when he was in his late twenties. It didn't work out," he said with a grimace. "Thankfully the union didn't produce any children."

"What do you mean? Shawn wouldn't make a good father?"

Win shook his head. "No. Because the marriage didn't last but about two years. It's not easy to raise kids on your own and, if they'd had children, I figure Shawn would've had to take on the major load of parenting. Anyway, I don't think he cares if he ever marries again."

And what about him? Had he decided he didn't want to be a husband for a second time? Even though she wanted to ask the questions, Stacy realized it was far too soon for her to pry into such a private subject. Besides, the boys were sitting close enough to hear every word that was said.

"I'm sorry for your brother. I remember what an awful time my brother Billy and his kids went through when he and his first wife got a divorce," she said soberly then purposely gave him a cheerful smile. "But as you might've noticed the other night, he and Charlotte are incredibly happy now. So, your brother shouldn't give up on finding happiness. And neither should you."

And what about herself? Was she truly happy? Stacy

hadn't really asked herself that question until recently—until she'd met Win. Before their paths had crossed, she'd mostly focused on her teaching job and pushed the personal side of her life to the back of her mind. When she did allow herself to think of becoming a wife and mother, she told herself to be patient and it would happen. But this past year she had to admit her hopes had dimmed.

She noticed his eyes had narrowed as he continued to study her face and Stacy got the impression he resented her remark.

"What makes you think I'm not happy?"

He didn't appear to be all that annoyed with her, but the clipped tone of his words said otherwise. Still, she wasn't about to apologize.

"I didn't mean you weren't happy," she said. "I only meant that you…well, you're still a very young man and have a lot to look forward to."

His lips twisted. "Very young? I'm twelve years older than you."

"That doesn't change the fact that you're still a very young man," she told him.

The twist to his lips changed from mocking to amused. "You're not wearing glasses, so you must be wearing rose-colored contacts."

She laughed. "Hardly. My vision is perfect."

"Hey, Dad, I'm finished eating." Joshua spoke up. "Is it okay if I go now? Katrina might be looking for me."

"Sure," Win told him. "We'll hang around the park for a little longer. I'll look you up when I'm ready to go."

Stacy reached inside the picnic basket and pulled out a flat plastic container with a lid. "Here, Joshua. Take a brownie with you. Or take two. Katrina might like one."

The teenagers face lit up. "Oh, brownies! Thanks, Ms. Abernathy!"

She wrapped two of the desserts in a napkin and after she handed them to Joshua, he took off in a trot to the other side of the park.

His face a picture of bewilderment, Oliver stared after his brother. "He sure is acting weird today. You think he's getting sick, Dad?"

Win and Stacy exchanged knowing smiles.

"He's not sick," Win assured the boy. "He's just growing up a little today."

Oliver drew back his shoulders in an effort to appear taller. "Am I growing today?"

Stacy wanted to laugh but managed to hold her reaction to a broad smile while Win gave her a conspiring wink.

He said, "You're growing every day, Oliver. And you'll keep on growing until you become a man."

His expression skeptical, Oliver asked, "Do you think I'll get to be as tall as you are, Dad?"

Win gave his son an indulgent smile. "Probably taller. Especially after the way you've eaten so much of Stacy's food. I think you and Joshua have eaten everything she had in the basket."

"Gosh, Dad, that's why she brought the food. So we could eat it."

Win slanted Stacy a wry look. "It's a good thing you showed up or my boys would've starved," he joked.

"I came prepared," she said simply. He didn't need to know she'd purposely asked her mother to prepare extra food just in case she had a chance to invite him to share her lunch. Win wasn't a man who'd appreciate being chased by a woman and she hardly wanted to give him the impression that she was running after him.

Oliver stood and rubbed a hand over his stomach. "I still have room for a brownie," he said to Stacy. "Could I take one to Artie, too?" he asked.

"I think it's very nice of you to think of Artie." Stacy reached for the container and, after wrapping two more brownies, she handed them to Oliver.

"Thanks! This is great!" He took off in a run then put on the brakes and looked back at Win. "Me and Artie will be over on the playground with Leo."

"Who's Leo?" Win wanted to know.

"His dog! Bye!"

Oliver raced away and Win took off his hat and ran a weary hand through his hair. "I imagine your head is spinning."

Stacy laughed softly. "Are you kidding? I hear kids chattering all day long. And I'm glad to see your sons enjoying themselves. But there is something I'm curious about, Win. Do you not allow your sons to have cell phones? Nearly every child I see has one. Even some of my second graders have dragged them out of their backpacks while in class and then, of course, I have to confiscate them. It's a difficult thing for parents to deal with."

"When Joshua turned thirteen, I let him get a phone. But it's only to use for calls to his family or friends at the appropriate time. It's not equipped for surfing the web. I'm not going to allow that sort of thing until he gets somewhat older. At times, he gripes that I'm an old fogey but, for the most part, I don't hear much complaining. As for Oliver, he couldn't care less about a phone. He'd rather be outside playing with the dogs or cats."

"Sounds like you're being fair and wise," she said with an approving nod. "I should've known."

He let out a low, mocking grunt. "My sons wouldn't always agree to the fair part. But it's nice to hear you say it. To be honest, both boys expected this picnic to be boring. They thought it was going to be a bunch of teachers sitting around talking shop. They didn't think any of their friends would be here. In fact, they made me promise I wouldn't keep them here at the picnic for very long." He let out a short laugh. "If I tried to take them home now, I'd hear all kinds of squawking."

His hand was resting on his knee and she couldn't stop herself from reaching over and touching her fingers to his. The warmth of his skin matched the glimmer in his eyes and, as their gazes locked, a strange flutter struck the pit of her stomach.

She inhaled a deep breath and slowly released it. "I'm glad," she murmured. "It's nice to have your company."

"That goes both ways, Stacy. It's nice to be with you."

His voice had lowered to a rough murmur and the sexy sound caused a nervous lump to enter her throat. She swallowed then swallowed again before she ventured to speak. "Uh...after I put away this food, would you like to walk around the park? It might actually be a little quieter on the far end—away from the picnic tables."

"Sounds good," he said. "I'll help you pack up these things."

At Stacy's car, Win placed the picnic basket filled with the remnants of their lunch onto the back floorboard and, after she tossed the blanket onto the seat, she punched a button on the door to relock the vehicle.

"Now that we've cleaned the kitchen," she said with an impish grin, "we can explore some of the park. Have you ever been here before today?"

"I've driven by a few times, but never stopped," he admitted.

"Good. Then maybe you won't be too bored."

"I doubt that will happen." Not with her company, he thought.

They moved away from the parking area and, as they began walking across a wide expanse of lawn, Win instinctively reached for her hand and tugged her closer to his side. She didn't resist his touch. In fact, the smile she flashed up at him said she enjoyed being close to him and Win wondered if he was losing his senses.

He didn't want to get involved with this woman. Sure, she was sweet and pretty. And judging by the beans and brownies she'd cooked for the picnic, she could cook. But he didn't need a cook. After all these years without a wife, he was fairly adept at putting a meal together. Besides, Stacy was the marrying kind of woman, not the casual affair sort. And he didn't need her, or any woman, putting a rope around him and tugging him down the marriage aisle.

What about needing her in your bed, Win? Have you forgotten how long and empty your nights have been? Wouldn't having her warm arms around you be worth putting a ring on her finger?

The taunting questions traipsing through his head should've been enough to make him release his hold on her hand and put a cool and sensible distance between them. But having her close to him was like hot coffee on a cold night. He didn't want to give up the pleasure before the cup was empty.

"Mmm. The breeze is just right. It's a perfect day." She looked up at the sky where a few clouds were scudding from north to south. "What I love about the park at this time of the year is the trees. The bright-colored leaves of the hardwoods look so beautiful next to the evergreens."

His gaze drifted away from the tempting line of her neck to where her attention was cast on a row of trees outlining the far end of the park.

"The leaves are starting to turn on the J Barb, too. The cottonwood in front of the house is a bright yellow now. I have to admit it's beautiful." It was on the tip of his tongue to suggest she come over and see the tree for herself, but he stopped the words from slipping past his lips. Why get entangled in a relationship that could never work? He'd be asking for trouble. And yet the empty holes in him were crying for him to reach for any kind of happiness she might give him. No matter how short-lived.

She sighed. "Sounds lovely."

Not nearly as lovely as her, Win thought as his gaze swept over her sun-kissed face. He couldn't ever remember seeing skin like hers. It was so fine and smooth, he couldn't spot one single pore. No doubt it would feel like silk against his cheek, beneath his lips.

He cleared his throat. "Yes, but the beauty doesn't last long. Then we're staring at bare limbs for several months."

A faint smile tilted the corners of her lips and Win wondered what she might do if he suddenly pulled her into his arms and kissed her. Would she curtly remind him that they were both teachers at a public function and had to behave with decorum?

He was still imagining the kiss when she said, "I'll tell you something else that looks beautiful at this time of the year. The huge pumpkin patch at the Bronco Harvest Festival. It's especially beautiful at night with the moon shining on everything."

Had she ever visited the pumpkin patch in the moonlight

with a man at her side? With her looks and social status in the community, Win figured there'd been plenty of guys lined up at her door, but she never mentioned dating. And when Anthony had found out about Win having dinner at the Bonnie B, his coworker had remarked that he couldn't recall Stacy ever having a serious boyfriend. She'd told Win she'd not yet married because she was going to be particular, yet he couldn't help but wonder if there was another reason for her remaining single. A broken heart? A love that was never returned? He wanted to ask her about her past dating life, but if he did, she might get the idea he was getting seriously interested. And that would be misleading. He wasn't about to wander down that path again.

Pushing aside the rambling thoughts, he said, "It sounds as though I'm going to have to take the boys to the festival and the Gold Buckle Rodeo. I'm sure they'd enjoy both of them, plus I want them to feel like they're a part of Bronco's culture."

Her expression curious, she asked, "Did Joshua and Oliver like the idea of moving here to Bronco? Or would they rather have remained in Whitehorn?"

Win shrugged and hoped she wouldn't notice how uncomfortable her question had made him. Not that he had anything to hide from her or anyone. It was just that the ordeal he'd gone through with Tara still had enough sting to embarrass him. And he wasn't at all sure how Stacy would view the situation. There'd been friends and family who'd called him a coward for moving away from the only place he'd ever lived. And maybe a part of him had been a coward, he thought. Maybe, if he'd been a stronger man, he would've stood up and defended himself against Tara's trash talk. But, ultimately, he'd decided moving far away would fix the problem.

"At first, they weren't too keen on the idea. Especially moving away from their grandparents. But, thankfully, both boys started to view the move as an adventure and now I'm happy to say they love it here. In the end, I think it's best that they're not living in the same house as they lived with their mother. Reminders of her were all around the place and they kept her death fresh in Joshua's mind especially. And mine, too," he admitted.

"Had you and Yvette lived all your married life on the ranch?" she asked.

"Yes. I'd purchased the place before I asked Yvette to marry me. At that time, it wasn't much more than a piece of land with a house on it. So we built it into a ranch together."

"Oh my. No wonder the place held so many memories." A pained looked crossed her face as she gently squeezed his fingers. "I hope living in Bronco helps dim the loss for all of you."

The tenderness he saw in her eyes caused his chest to swell with an emotion he didn't quite understand. He tried to tell himself it was simply gratitude, but he knew the feeling was more than gratefulness.

"Hey, Stacy! Win!"

A female voice calling out their names caused them to pause and look around to see Robin and Dylan hurrying forward.

"Hi, you two!" Stacy said when the pair finally reached them.

Robin gave Stacy a brief hug as Dylan shook hands with Win.

Robin patted the picnic basket Dylan was carrying. "We're going to have lunch with Dante and Eloise. They should be around here somewhere."

Stacy said, "We ran into them earlier when we were chatting with the other elementary teachers."

"They're probably chasing after Merry. She loves being outdoors," Dylan said. "Would you two like to join us for lunch?"

Win groaned and rubbed his midsection. "I'm stuffed. Stacy shared her lunch with me and the boys."

Robin's brows lifted ever so slightly as she turned a smug sort of smile on her husband.

Win figured the woman was thinking there was something brewing between him and Stacy, which wouldn't exactly be wrong. From the moment she'd first walked up to him here in the park, he'd felt undercurrents of electricity flowing between them. But if he had any sense at all, he wouldn't allow the sparks to ignite a fire.

"We would've been here earlier," Dylan explained. "But Uncle Stanley asked me to make a few phones calls for him this morning—to see if anyone had any new news about Winona."

"Has anyone heard anything new?" Stacy asked.

Robin sadly shook her head while Dylan frowned.

"Unfortunately, no," Dylan answered. "And I'm getting extremely worried about Uncle Stanley. If Winona doesn't show up soon, or we don't get some kind of word from her, I'm afraid he's going to have a mental breakdown."

"I'm worried, too." Robin added to her husband's concern. "If he isn't pacing, he's staring off into space, imagining the worst. I feel so sorry for him. But there isn't much anybody can do. Every lead has been exhausted and there are no new clues to her whereabouts."

"Stanley must be wildly in love with Winona," Win said.

Robin said, "Their relationship was deep and genuine.

That's why no one can believe Winona simply ran away with cold feet."

"I have to believe Winona will be found safe," Stacy replied. "Bronco isn't the same without her. Just think of all the couples she helped to get engaged and married."

Win shot her a puzzled look and Dylan snickered.

"Is Winona some sort of matchmaker?" Win asked. "I thought she was supposed to be a psychic."

Robin said, "Winona can see things about people that normal folks can't see. She just intuitively seemed to know who should be matched together."

Win didn't bother to hide his skepticism. "Don't tell me she sprinkled some sort of magic love dust over these couples. I won't believe it."

Both Robin and Stacy laughed while Dylan shook his head with amusement.

"Nothing so obvious," Dylan told him. "She planted ideas and gave little nudges. That's all."

"And that's one of the many reasons we need for her to come home," Robin added. "So she can plant more ideas and nudge more folks toward happiness."

"Well, tell Stanley not to worry," Stacy said. "And that we're all praying for Winona's safe return."

Dylan assured Stacy he'd pass on the message and, after talking for a couple more minutes, the husband and wife said goodbye and headed to the opposite end of the park to search for Dante and Eloise.

Stacy and Win continued on their walk toward a grove of trees. As they strolled over the dormant grass, Win returned to the subject of Winona.

"Do you really believe Winona makes a man and woman fall in love?" he asked.

"Not at all."

Her unexpected answer caused him to pause and stare at her in wonder. "I don't get it. Not more than five minutes ago, you were saying she helped couples get engaged and married."

"That's true. She did. I could probably name you several couples that would thank Winona for nudging them in the right direction. But she doesn't *make* people fall in love. They do that on their own. At least that's how I imagine it will be for me."

His lips took on a wry slant. "Are you saying you've never been in love? That's hard to believe."

"Oh, there were times when I was younger that I thought I was in love. But later I realized it wasn't the deep feelings that truly defines love and all it means." She looked at him. "Did you know when you fell in love with Yvette?"

A few days ago, her question would have irked the hell out of him. He'd always considered his feelings for Yvette as private and, after she'd died, he especially hadn't wanted people digging into something that was none of their business. But something had apparently changed in him since he'd met Stacy. Now, he didn't resent her question. In fact, he understood her curiosity.

"It wasn't like a bolt out of the blue struck me. Our feelings grew gradually," he said gently.

Her eyes softened to a dreamy blue. "Instant or gradual it has to be magic."

He breathed deeply then urged her forward. "Yeah. Something like magic."

She didn't make any sort of reply and they continued to walk with their hands entwined. When they finally reached the grove, the sounds of the milling crowd were too far away to be heard and the branches of the evergreens created a screen of privacy.

"This is nice," Win said as he glanced around the cozy stand of trees. "I wonder why we're the only ones here at this end of the park."

Laughing lightly, she joked, "Because we're the only antisocial people here today." Her expression turned serious as she lifted her gaze up to his face. "Or maybe we're the only ones who appreciate being alone. At least, I enjoy being alone with you."

The glint in her eyes and breathless rush in her voice tugged on his senses and before he could stop himself, Win placed a hand on her shoulder and urged her deeper into the hanging branches of a huge fir.

Once he was certain they were hidden from view, he lowered his head until his face was mere inches away from hers. "Stacy, you're so lovely," he whispered. "And I've wanted to kiss you for so long."

She angled her face up to his. "And I've wanted you to kiss me, too."

His lips settled onto hers and a helpless groan rattled in his throat as lights flashed behind his closed eyes and his mind went momentarily blank. It wasn't until he felt her lips part and her palms flatten against the middle of his chest that he became fully aware of what he was doing. By then her soft, sweet lips were moving eagerly against his, inviting him to deepen the kiss.

Hot desire rushed from his loins to his brain and, without thinking, he pulled her into the tight circle of his arms. At the same time, he felt her body pressing itself closer, burning him with a need he'd long forgot.

Whether the kiss went on for long minutes or just a few seconds, Win couldn't say. He was only sure that he didn't want the contact of their lips to end. He didn't want to give up the heat flowing from her body and spreading through every cold, empty spot inside him.

When their lips finally eased apart, Win was so starved for oxygen, he turned his head aside and gulped in huge breaths of air. But replenishing his lungs did little to clear his senses. Everything around them was a spinning blur.

"Win," she whispered, "I didn't know it would be like this. So good."

His vision cleared just enough to see she was gazing up at him and the desire he saw flickering in the blue depths was enough to draw his mouth back down to hers.

Brushing his lips back and forth over hers, he whispered, "Too good."

This time when he kissed her, he wasn't expecting to find the same sizzle. But if anything, the connection was even hotter. In only a matter of seconds, he was totally lost in the softness of her lips and the sweet, mysterious taste of her. When his tongue pushed past her teeth and into the warm, moist cavity of her mouth, she reacted by curling her arms tightly around his neck. The shift in her body position caused her breasts to press against his chest and suddenly the need to make love to her was the only thought left in his brain.

It wasn't until a gust of wind caused one of the fir branches to lash against his shoulder that he managed to find the will to put an end to the fiery kiss and put some distance between their bodies.

Her expression dazed, she asked, "Win, I— Did I do something wrong?"

Stunned and embarrassed that he'd completely lost his control, he quickly turned his back to her and wiped a hand over his face.

"No. You did everything right," he said hoarsely. "That's

why—well, for a minute there, I sort of forgot we were in a public park with a group of people not far away. I hope no one happened to walk by and see us."

Her hand came to rest in the middle of his back and, for one wild second, Win considered saying to hell with it all and pulling her back into his arms. But now was not the time or the place to let his sexual urges get out of hand. Where Stacy was concerned, there wouldn't be a right time or place for sex.

Sex? Who was he kidding? What he'd just shared with Stacy went far beyond physical pleasure. Kissing her had taken him on a magical journey and he'd felt things that he'd never experienced with Yvette or any woman. What did it mean? What *could* it mean?

"Don't worry. No one can see us where we're standing. Anyway, what if they did? We're both single adults. There's nothing wrong with us kissing."

She called that kissing? He'd thought they'd been on the verge of making love!

Straightening his shoulders, he said, "No. I suppose not. But I—" He broke off as he turned and reached for her arm. "I think we'd better head back. I need to find the boys and get home to the J Barb."

With a hand beneath her elbow, he started to guide her out of the stand of evergreens, but she stuck her heels in the ground and refused to budge.

"Just a minute, Win. I want to ask you something, and I expect you to be honest with me."

The stubborn set to her jaw told him she wasn't all that happy about his abrupt announcement. But he couldn't very well admit that having her in his arms and kissing her sweet lips had shaken him to the very core of his being. Or that he'd never felt so much searing intensity in any kiss before.

"All right," he said. "What's your question?"

Her gaze flickered but never left his face. "Are you sorry you kissed me?"

He stared at her in stunned fascination. "Did I behave like a man under duress?"

Her lips flattened to a thin line. "You didn't answer me. You asked a question."

A strange mix of emotions suddenly balled in his throat. This woman was doing things to him he didn't understand and it scared the hell out of him.

He sighed heavily. "Okay, since you want to know, then no. I'm not sorry. Why would you think that?"

"Maybe it has something to do with the look of sick regret on your face," she said glumly then instantly shook her head. "Forget I said that. Forget I even asked the question. It doesn't matter."

He didn't know why, but suddenly her feelings meant far more to him than any concerns he had over making a fool of himself.

Cupping his hand against the side of her face, he said, "Oh, Stacy. It does matter. And I think...well, you should know that kissing you was—it couldn't have been any better. I just think it would be best for both of us if we...slowed down a bit."

She closed her eyes as her lips tilted into a wry smile. "Yes. I understand."

"Do you really?"

Her blue eyes opened and looked directly into his. "Yes. You're not an impulsive person and neither am I. Slow and steady is the way we need to handle things between us. That's what you're saying. Right?"

"Yeah. Right."

Everything she'd just said was dead-on right. So why did

he want to pull her back into the shadows of the trees and make love to her? Because he was lonely? Because living without a woman for all these years had left him feeling like only half a man?

Shutting his mind to those nagging questions, he placed a soft kiss in the center of her forehead and then ushered her out of the grove of the trees.

As they walked toward the busy picnic area, Stacy glanced up at the darkening sky. "Oh my, those clouds rolling in look ominous."

From the first moment he'd walked up to this woman in the hallway of the elementary school, he'd felt threatening clouds gathering over his head. Now he could only wonder how long he had before the storm actually hit.

"Yeah. Looks like it's time for us to go home," he replied.

And try to forget the brief passion they'd shared in the grove of evergreens.

Chapter Six

The following Monday, during afternoon recess, Stacy and Emma sat together on a cement bench located at one end of the playground, while the students from first and second grades released energy by swinging on several gym sets and playing tag on a wide expanse of grassy lawn.

"That was quite a rainstorm that hit the back-to-school picnic," Emma commented. "I'm just glad most everyone had eaten before scrambling for shelter. I got drenched. Did you?"

"No. I left before the rain started."

Curious, Emma looked at her. "Oh. I'd thought you might come back by our table to chat a while. But after you went to say hello to Win, I never saw you again."

Win. Even though two days had passed since she'd told him goodbye at the park, her mind was still obsessing over the man. The more time they'd spent together, the more she'd been drawn to him. By the time he'd pulled her into the thick grove of evergreens, all she'd wanted was to hold him close to her, to kiss every hard angle of his mouth and to show him how much he was beginning to mean to her. And for those short moments she'd spent in his arms, she'd believed he was feeling the same way about her. But, obviously, she'd misjudged the hot kisses he'd placed upon her lips.

When they'd parted at the picnic, she been practically holding her breath, hoping he would say he wanted to see her again, perhaps even ask her on a real date. But he'd not even offered to give her a call. So much for holding his interest, she thought glumly.

Sighing, she said, "I tell you, Emma, I honestly can't figure what Win is thinking."

Emma's expression turned wry. "I presume you're talking about what he's thinking about you."

"Yes," she mumbled, giving her head a hopeless shake. "At times, he seems like he's interested in me and then, just when I begin to feel hopeful, he goes all cool and distant. I might as well face it, when it comes to men, I'm a loser."

Instead of sympathizing with her, Emma laughed out loud. "Stacy, you must be half blind. What do you see when you look at yourself in the mirror? If you're not seeing a beautiful woman, then something is terribly wrong with you."

Frowning, Stacy looked away from her friend and out to the running and shrieking kids. Thankfully, the group continued to play without any arguments or skinned elbows or knees.

"Emma, it takes more than a nice appearance to hold a man. Especially one like Win. I think the way a person looks is secondary to him. He's more about personality, and mine must be boring as heck."

"So, what you're really saying is that you thought he'd ask to see you again and he hasn't. Right?"

Nodding, Stacy said, "Go ahead. Tell me I set my sights too high. I mean you know what the guy looks like. He could have most any woman he wanted."

Emma grimaced. "Have you stopped to think the man has been a widower for several years? Could be he doesn't want a woman in his life. Not a steady one, at least."

But when Win had kissed her, she could've sworn she'd felt desire on his lips. He was definitely capable of wanting a woman, she thought. But apparently he'd not wanted Stacy. Not enough to enter a relationship with her.

Still, she'd give her friend the benefit of the doubt. "You could be right, Emma. Besides, I shouldn't be asking for miracles."

Emma reached over and gave the back of Stacy's hand a motherly pat. "Look, Stacy, Win had dinner with you and your family on the Bonnie B. And the two of you shared lunch at the school picnic. That hardly sounds like a man who's disinterested. Anyway, he might be waiting on you to ask him out."

Stacy's jaw dropped and just as she was about to tell Emma she wasn't the man-chasing kind, the sound of the bell announced the end of the recess period.

Both women rose to their feet and began lining up the young students for an orderly march back inside the building. But even as Stacy dealt with her lively second graders, she was thinking about Win and wondering if Emma could be right. Maybe he was waiting on Stacy to make the next move. And if he was, did she have the courage to make it?

"Remember, students, tomorrow afternoon is the field trip to the farm and ranch supply store," Win told his last class of the day. "For those of you who are planning to go, be sure to bring the permission slip your parent signed. For those of you who don't choose to go, I'll have something for you to study on the subject of budgeting and utilizing supplies for farming and ranching."

"I already have my permission note, Mr. Jackson. Can I give it to you now?"

Win looked toward the back of the room, where a tall, male student with carrot-colored hair was waving a small slip of paper in the air.

"Yes, I'll take it, Clete. Is there anyone else who wants to turn in their permissions slips today?" he asked.

Several students immediately held up their slips and Win walked around the room collecting them. He'd just taken the last one from a cheeky boy with a face full of freckles when the final bell rang to dismiss school for the day.

While backpacks were retrieved from beneath desks and kids called to each other as they quickly shuffled out the door, Win returned to his desk and began to gather the papers he intended to work on later tonight.

"Excuse me, Mr. Jackson. Can I ask you a question?"

He glanced up to see the last student in the room had paused at the corner of his desk. Julie was a petite girl with dark hair and a shy demeanor. So far, she'd been an excellent pupil, but Win had the feeling her life away from school was a struggle.

"Sure," he said. "What's your question?"

She nodded. "I was wondering if you're going to mark down grades for the students who don't go on the field trip tomorrow."

He studied her solemn face. "No. I won't be doing anything like that. I'll allow those students to make up their studies in some other way. Is there a special reason you're asking?"

Her gaze dropped to the floor as she fidgeted nervously with the shoulder strap of her handbag. "Well, I don't want to get a poor grade."

"You don't plan on joining us for the field trip tomorrow?"

"No," she mumbled. "I want to go—really bad. But my dad won't let me. He says I don't have any business leaving the school grounds."

Dealing with overprotective parents was hardly anything new for Win. Over the years he'd been teaching, he'd encountered plenty. But he had the feeling that Julie's home situation was more than an obsessive parent, and the idea bothered him greatly.

"Did you assure him that there would be plenty of chaperones with the group?"

She looked glumly up at him and shrugged both shoulders. "I tried. But he didn't care to hear about that."

Win thought for a moment before he suggested, "I'd be glad to call and talk to him if you think that would help."

A look of pure distress pinched the girl's features. "Oh no! Please don't! He, uh, isn't well. And he doesn't want to talk on the phone."

Because the man drank and wanted to hide it, Win wondered. Or was her father actually too sick to feel like holding a conversation? As Julie's teacher, it would be helpful to know the situation, but Win didn't want to embarrass the girl by asking her outright. "I see," he said and then carefully asked, "Does your mother live with you, or in town? I'd be happy to call her if you think it would help."

"She lives far away in Nevada. I don't see her very often."

Looking at this subdued child, Win had to wonder what his life would've been like if one of his children had been a daughter. Without Yvette to help him with parenting a little girl, he would've been lost.

"Well, it's okay, Julie. You're one of my best students. Don't worry about the field trip or anything else. However, if you need to talk to me for any reason, all you have to do is ask. Will you remember that?"

She gave him a timid smile. "Yes. I'll remember. Thank you, Mr. Jackson."

Win watched her leave the classroom while wishing there was more he could do for her. But, sadly, Julie wasn't the only student in Bronco High School whose home life was far from ideal. Win couldn't fix everything for those children. All he could do was teach the ones in his agriculture classes to the best of his ability and hope the lessons they learned would eventually help to give each of them a better life.

Picking up the canvas duffel bag he'd loaded with test papers and lesson plans, he left the room and walked down a long hallway until he reached an exit leading out of the building. As usual, he was running late and, as he headed to the teachers' parking lot, he expected to find Joshua already in the truck and waiting.

As he rounded a row of hedge and started down a long sidewalk to the parking area, he glanced toward his truck parked several yards away, then stopped in his tracks. His son was definitely waiting at the truck, but he wasn't alone. Katrina, the girl Joshua had introduced to him and Stacy at the school picnic, was standing next to him. And judging from the wide smile on his face, she must have been saying all the right things.

How had this little romance happened so quickly? Win wondered. Ever since Joshua's girlfriend in Whitehorn had dropped him, the boy had sworn off girls. Obviously, Katrina had managed to change his mind.

Like Stacy is changing yours?

The nagging question was rattling around in Win's head when he heard a familiar voice behind him.

"Hey, Win, wait up a minute."

Turning, he saw Anthony striding up the sidewalk. Dressed in gray gym clothes and a baseball cap, he'd clearly just come from a PE class.

Win waited until his friend was standing next to him before he said, "I've not seen you around the past couple of days. Where have you been?"

"Busy. I guess you haven't heard. I'm assisting the basketball coach now. Ronnie, his regular assistant, is laid up with a broken leg, so I had to take his place."

"No. I hadn't heard about Ronnie. What about your PE classes?"

"I'm doing those, too. And I'm dog-tired, that's what," Anthony told him. "And today has been one of those days best forgotten. I figure I deserve to take myself out for pizza tonight and I thought you and the boys might like to join me. My treat."

"Thanks for asking, Anthony. But I need to get home. I've been having trouble with an automatic valve on one of my watering troughs. I need to work on it before dark."

"Darn. Well, we'll make it another night then. That is, unless you're too busy seeing Stacy," he added slyly.

Win frowned at the younger man. "What are you talking about? I'm not seeing Stacy."

A smug grin crossed Anthony's face. "Could've fooled me. I saw you two walking everywhere together at the park last Saturday. And you looked pretty chummy. I imagined you would've already asked her out on a date by now."

Win came close to muttering a curse. For the past three days, Oliver had been hounding him about seeing Stacy. Now, Anthony had joined in. It was too much. Especially when he'd been trying like hell to get her and those hot kisses out of his mind.

"You figured wrong," he said stiffly.

Anthony looked puzzled. "Why? She's nice, and pretty. What's the matter? Is she too chatty for you?"

Talk wasn't the problem, Win thought as he stifled a helpless groan. Kissing was the crux of the matter. She made him feel and want things he'd not thought about for a long time. She made him dream and wish for all the things he'd lost when his wife had died. It wasn't right. It wasn't good. Yvette was the one love of his life. Why try to have another one?

Exhaling a weighted breath, he said, "No. I like Stacy. A lot. I just don't think now is the time to get involved with a woman."

Anthony's eyebrow arched. "You sound like a damned fool. When would be the right time? When you get old and the boys are grown and gone from home?" he asked with a heavy dose of sarcasm. "I'd call that wasting some good years."

"Look, Anthony, I know you mean well, but you don't understand. I told you all about the misery Tara caused me when I called it quits with her. I don't want to go through that kind of headache again."

Anthony leveled a pointed look at him. "You're right. I can't understand completely because I've not lost a wife like you have. Hell, I've not even had a wife to lose. But if you're worried that Stacy could be another Tara, you're delusional. You really want to know what I think?"

Rolling his eyes, Win glanced at his watch. "I think you're making me later than I already am."

He took off walking in the direction of his truck, but instead of being put off, Anthony stuck to his side. "You're going to hear what I think anyway. I don't believe you're a bit worried about Stacy behaving like Tara. What you're really worried about is loving her and losing her."

Win's boots practically skidded on the graveled surface as he stopped abruptly and turned to face Anthony. "Hell, yes, that worries me! Wouldn't it worry you?"

Anthony shook his head. "Life is too short to live in fear. If I had the opportunity you have with a woman like Stacy, I wouldn't be wasting it cowering at home, chewing on my nails."

"You're a real friend, Anthony." Win sneered.

The other man chuckled. "Why do you think I'm giving you a lecture? Because you're my friend and I want you to be happy."

Win swiped a hand over his face then glanced over to where Joshua and Katrina were still talking. His son was now holding the girl's hand and the sight of their young and tender relationship caused a pang of bittersweet emotion to slice through his chest. Win was glad Joshua had found a special someone. But how would his son handle things if his heart was broken a second time?

Forget about a second broken heart, Win. Think about the miserable life your son would have if he was afraid to love. Like you.

The little voice came from out of the blue and struck Win like a thunderbolt. He was being a coward. His own teenaged son had more courage than he did.

He let out a heavy sigh. "Yeah. I know you want me to be happy, Anthony. And I understand a person has to take chances in life if he's ever going to get the most out of it. So I'm…going to try."

Anthony gave Win's shoulder a friendly slap. "Now you're talking, buddy."

Giving his friend a lopsided grin, Win asked, "Why

don't you come out to the ranch tonight? I have some frozen pizza I can bake. I might even find a beer to go with it. The boys would enjoy your company."

"I don't even have to think about an offer like that. I'll be there. What time?"

"Come early. You can help me with the water float."

Anthony chuckled. "I knew there must be a catch in there somewhere. Okay. I'll drive over after I go home and change."

The two men parted and Win waited long enough for Joshua to give Katrina a quick goodbye before he drove the two of them away from the school building.

"Wow, Dad, you're late! Oliver might be locked out of the building!" Joshua exclaimed.

Win pressed down on the accelerator while keeping a cautious eye on the speedometer. Getting a speeding ticket would only make things worse. "I'm not that late. There's usually a teacher or two who stay after the last bell."

"Like Ms. Abernathy?" Joshua asked.

Win silently groaned. Ever since the three of them had shared Stacy's picnic lunch last Saturday, his sons had been making sly innuendos regarding the pretty teacher and their dad. As far as Oliver was concerned, he'd be thrilled if Win took Stacy on a date. As for Joshua, his older son appeared to be softening his opinion about women. But he wasn't sure how the teenager would view his father going on a date. Not that Win was planning such a thing, or that Stacy would agree to go out with him. No, as much as he'd been blown away by Stacy's kisses, he needed to keep a cool head and remember the reason he'd moved to Bronco in the first place.

"You and Oliver don't miss anything, do you?"

"We can tell that you like her," Joshua answered.

"I do like Stacy," Win said frankly. "Probably as much as you like Katrina."

A glance in the rearview mirror showed Joshua scooting as far up in the seat as the shoulder harness would allow. "Gosh, Dad, I really like Katrina. I even kissed her at the school picnic. And you know what?"

Win tried not to appear shocked, even though his head was spinning at the thought that he'd not been the only Jackson male to do some kissing at the school picnic.

"No. What?" Win asked.

"She kissed me back. And it was awesome!"

Another glance in the mirror revealed a big grin on Joshua's face. "That's the way it is, son, when you're with a girl you really like."

"Yeah, Katrina is a lot nicer than Monica back in Whitehorn," Joshua said, letting out a contented sigh. "Dad, I'm really glad we moved here to Bronco. Aren't you?"

In the beginning, when they'd first arrived in Bronco, there had been days that Win had questioned himself over the move. He'd wondered if he'd done the right thing by uprooting himself and the boys. And wondered, too, if they would fit in with the locals. Nowadays, he didn't wonder any more. He just thanked God that he'd made the move.

"Yes, I am," he told Joshua. "It feels like home."

Joshua leaned up closer to Win's shoulder. "You know, Dad, if you really like Stacy—I mean, Ms. Abernathy, you ought to kiss her. I bet you'd like it."

Win's foot very nearly slipped off the accelerator. He'd liked it, all right. So much so that he still couldn't get her or the kisses they'd shared out of his mind.

Clearing his throat, he said, "I imagine kissing Stacy would be nice. But a grown man doesn't go around kissing a woman just because he'd like to. Older women have different ideas about such things."

"Aww, shoot. If that's the way it is, then I'd rather just stay fifteen and not have to worry about all those other things."

Yes, things had been a lot simpler when Win had been fifteen. He'd not known then that he'd be raising two sons without his wife at his side. He'd not imagined that the idea of loving a second time would fill him with cold dread. When he thought about Stacy, he wished he could be young and innocent again. He wished he could start over with a heart full of love and trust.

Five minutes later, when he parked in front of the elementary school, Oliver and three other children were waiting on the steps at the front entrance of the building. Carrie Waters was there to make sure each one left with their authorized ride.

As soon as he'd hustled Oliver into the truck and pulled away from the school parking lot, his son let out a disappointed groan.

"You shouldn't have been so late, Dad. Ms. Abernathy had been waiting out on the steps with Carrie for a long time before she finally got in her car and drove off. You could've talked to her. I know she wanted to see you."

Joshua thought his father ought to be kissing Stacy while Oliver thought he should be talking with her. What was going on with his sons anyway?

"What makes you think she wanted to see me?" Win asked him. "Did she tell you that?"

"Well, no. Not exactly. But she did ask how you were doing. I told her I'd tell you to call her."

Win wearily pinched the bridge of his nose and tried not to groan out loud. "Okay, you've told me. Now, that's enough about Stacy. We're going to have company tonight. Anthony is coming over to eat pizza with us. And I want the both of you to be on your best behavior."

A glance in the mirror showed Joshua making a triumphant fist pump; which was hardly surprising. Anthony was one of the first people they'd met when they'd moved to Bronco back in the early summer and since then both boys had grown very fond of the young athletic coach.

"Great!" he exclaimed. "Does that mean we get to stay up late?"

"No. It means you're going to wash all the dirty dishes tonight," Win informed the teenager.

When Joshua groaned in protest, Oliver began to giggle.

Glancing in the rearview mirror at the pair, Win said, "Don't be so quick to laugh, Oliver. You're going to help him."

Later that evening at the main ranch house, after the Abernathys had finished dinner, Stacy and Robin shooed their mother out of the kitchen and went to work loading the dishwasher and putting away the leftovers.

"I was planning to stay home and work on lesson plans, but when Mom called and told me you and Dylan would be here, I couldn't refuse the invite to join all of you," Stacy said as she placed a container of scalloped potatoes into the refrigerator. "I need to hear my sister tell me I'm making a fool of myself and then I might be able to do something about it."

Chuckling, Robin dunked a small copper stewing pot into a sink of sudsy water. "You've never made a fool of yourself. Why would you start now?"

Stacy shut the door on the refrigerator and walked over to stand next to her sister. "I've been asking myself that same question," she said. Then, shaking her head, she asked, "Wouldn't you say I'm usually a sensible person? That I'm not delusional trying to shoot for an impossible star?"

Robin rinsed the pot then handed it to Stacy for her to dry.

"I'd say you're one of the most levelheaded persons I know—even if you are my sister," she added impishly. "What's wrong, anyway? Did something happen at school to upset you?"

Corralling a room full of seven-year-olds while trying to teach them was a snap compared to dealing with the uncertainty she was feeling over Win, Stacy thought.

Sighing, Stacy opened a lower cabinet and placed the dried pot on a shelf. "This isn't about school. It's Win. I can't get him out of my mind. I'm worried that I'm falling for the man."

"Why should that worry you?" Robin asked with a quizzical frown. "Falling for a guy is nothing abnormal—it's actually wonderful. And let's be honest, Stacy. For you, this has been a long time coming."

Stacy bit down on her bottom lip as she glanced uncertainly at her sister. "If you're thinking I've been purposely avoiding falling in love because of Spence, you're wrong."

Robin grimaced. "I wasn't going to bring Spence into the conversation, because I know the memory of him makes you cringe."

"Of course it makes me cringe," Stacy said flatly. "He was the biggest mistake of my life. And after Spence all I've ever known is boring dates and men who leave me disinterested. How can I know what I'm feeling? The only thing I'm certain about is that I can't get Win out of my mind. And that can't be good."

Robin chuckled. "Stacy, you need to relax. Falling in

love is a little like being obsessed. But it's a glorious sort of obsession. Especially when your partner is equally moon-struck."

Try as she might, Stacy couldn't imagine Win losing his head over her, or any woman. "Win isn't the dreamy sort. At least, not with me," she said dully.

Robin pulled the strainer from the sink and reached for a dishtowel. "What makes you think he isn't? I saw the way he was holding your hand at the picnic."

Rolling her eyes, Stacy said, "You sound like Emma now. Today, during recess, she suggested Win might be waiting on me to make the first move and ask him out. Can you imagine me asking a man like him for a date?"

"No. Because you'd be too afraid he'd turn you down and then you'd be terribly embarrassed. Right?"

"It would be humiliating," Stacy admitted, tilting her head to one side as she continued to consider the idea. "You remember that guy who caught my eye in college? The one before I started dating Spence?"

"Vaguely. Nothing ever happened with the two of you."

Stacy grimaced. "Exactly my point. I was infatuated with him. And when I finally got up enough nerve to ask him to join me for coffee, he acted as though I'd insulted him. I wanted to crawl in a hole. But that humiliation wasn't enough to make me think twice about dating. It wasn't long after that experience that I met Spence and—well, we all know how that turned out. When it comes to men my judgement is definitely shaky."

Robin shook her head. "From what I see, Win isn't a bit like those guys. He's settled and responsible."

"Yes," Stacy agreed. "But I'm not at all sure he'd appreciate me inviting him on a date. Still, if I did ask Win and he turned me down, I don't suppose I'd be losing anything—other than my pride. Nothing ventured, nothing gained. Right?"

"Right." With a smile of encouragement, Robin gave her a hug then stepped back and leveled a serious look at her. "I'm just wondering, though, if you've carefully thought through getting involved with Win. He's somewhat older than you. And he has two sons, who are at the age where parenting starts to get difficult. The other night at the dinner table, I recall how the older boy flatly stated he didn't need or want a mother. Talk about a challenge. I'd really have to love the man in order to deal with that sort of resentment from his child."

Stacy sighed. "Trust me, Robin. I've thought about all those things. Especially the fact that Win is a widower and Joshua is still clinging to his mother's memory. But I— When I'm with Win, I feel like I want to take a risk and see if the two of us could have something special."

Robin's smile was understanding. "If that's the way you feel, then you should try to see him again. Then if the two of you click in the right way, everything else will fall into place."

If was a mighty big word and Robin had just used it twice, Stacy noted. Still, she wasn't ready to mark Win off as a lost cause. But were the two of them actually meant to be together? The answer to that question was something she had to find out for herself.

Chapter Seven

The next day, Win was even busier than usual with the afternoon field trip to the Bronco Farm and Ranch Supply store. But the outing turned out well and the students learned firsthand about the many common expenditures farmers and ranchers dealt with on a daily basis. That had been Win's main objective for the trip.

Just before the class had loaded onto the bus to leave for the trip, Win had handed out worksheets for the students who were staying behind in study hall. Julie had been one of them and when Win paused at the side of her desk, she'd stared soulfully in front of her rather than look up at him. He'd not questioned the girl again about her father. Rather than help the situation, he realized bringing up the issue a second time would only make her feel worse. He also realized Julie needed a mother in her life.

Oliver and Joshua need a mother, too. You can't do anything to help Julie, but you can damned well give your sons a mother.

The nagging voice in Win's head was a constant thing. So were his thoughts of Stacy. The time he'd spent with her at the school picnic had turned him into a daydreaming fool. No matter how hard he fought to push her out of his mind, he couldn't quit thinking about her kisses. He couldn't stop himself from wanting to hold and kiss her again.

"Dad, did you want me to give the horses the same amount of alfalfa tonight?"

Joshua's question interrupted Win's wandering thoughts and he glanced up to see the teenager had paused at the open doorway of the barn. Only a few minutes ago, he and the boys had arrived home from school and now the three of them were at the barn, taking care of the evening chores.

"Give them half a block extra this evening," Win told him. "The weather is getting colder and I don't see much grass left in the pasture for them to graze on."

"Okay. I got it," Joshua told him.

Off to the left of Win, two border collies were yipping with excitement as they ran tight circles around Oliver's legs. The task of feeding the dogs was something his younger son enjoyed, which explained Oliver's loud giggles as the pups playfully nipped at his heels.

"Oliver, be sure and fill the dogs' water tub," Win called to him. "I don't want them trying to jump up on the edge of the horses' water trough to get a drink. If one of them fell in, I'm not sure he could climb out."

Oliver gave his father an assuring wave. "Don't worry, Dad. I never forget the dogs' water."

Win gave the boy a thumbs-up then went on inside the barn where he had a sick cow and her calf penned in a stall. He'd just given the cow an injection of antibiotic and was pouring her a helping of feed into a rubber tub, when the cell phone in his pocket buzzed with an incoming call.

His first thought was to ignore it. He had a few more things around the ranch yard that needed his attention before dark. He didn't have time for a phone chat. But the possibility that the caller might be one of his parents, or his brother back in Whitehorn with important news, had him reaching for the phone.

The sight of Stacy's name and number on the ID momentarily stunned Win. Even though the two of them had exchanged phone numbers at the picnic, he'd not expected her to call any time soon. As for Win calling her, there had been several times during the past three days that he'd almost tapped her number. However, each time he'd told himself he'd be a fool to invite problems and had put the phone away.

Now his heart was suddenly racing as he clicked the accept button and held the phone to his ear. "Hi, Stacy. How are you?"

"I'm great," she said cheerfully. "Did I catch you at a bad time?"

"I'm just doing some chores at the barn. No big deal." The idea that he was trying to sound cool and casual caused him to silently curse. Since when did a forty-year-old man need to appear cool? After he'd let a woman turn him into a fool?

"Oh. I apologize for the interruption. I won't keep you long," she promised. "Uh, the reason I'm calling is... I wanted to invite you and the boys over to the Bonnie B tonight. That is, if you're able to finish your chores before too late. We've had a happy event take place over here and I wanted to share it with you. And have you three stay for dinner, of course."

After the family dinner he and the boys had shared with the Abernathys several days ago, Win had sworn it was the first and last. But things had changed drastically since then, he mentally argued. He and Stacy had gotten more acquainted. They'd also gotten close enough to exchange several hot kisses. And, anyway, he couldn't deny he'd been longing to see her again.

Smiling in spite of himself, he stepped out of the small pen holding the cow and calf and carefully latched the gate behind him. "A little happy news is always welcome. What's happened?"

"One of Dad's mares has foaled twins and they are absolutely adorable. I thought you and the boys would enjoy seeing them."

"Twins. That is a happy event. And rare," Win said. "I've heard of mares having twins, but never actually seen a set of them."

"Dad says he's never had a mare have twins before this one. You can imagine he's over the moon. Mom practically had to drag him away from the barn last night. The babies were born around nine and he wouldn't leave them until the vet arrived and declared the mare and foals to be healthy. And that ended up being around two this morning."

Win's mind was suddenly spinning. Not with the news of the twin foals, but with the fact that Stacy wanted to see him again. Still, going over to the Bonnie B might give her all the wrong signals. She might start thinking he was romantically interested in her.

And she'd be right, Win. You want like hell to see her again, too. Don't hem and haw and hide from the truth.

The taunting reprimand caused him to swipe a weary hand over his face. "Short night for your father. But I don't imagine he minded the loss of sleep."

She laughed softly. "Dad doesn't realize he's lost any sleep."

The joy he heard in her laughter had him thinking back to the school picnic and how happiness had showed on her face and twinkled in her blue eyes. He'd wanted to bottle up all her joy and use it later when the empty side of his bed caused an ache in his chest.

"Win? Are you still there?"

Giving himself a hard mental shake, he said. "I'm here. Uh, I guess you're waiting on an answer?"

"Well, yes. I need to let Mom know if she's having guests for dinner."

In spite of all the doubts and self-admonitions that had been going through Win's mind since he'd kissed her so wantonly, he couldn't stop a wave of eager excitement from rushing through him.

"Okay, Stacy. If you're certain you want us, we'll be over after we wrap up the chores."

He could hear a breath of air rush out of her. Had she been worried he'd turn her down?

"I'm so glad, Win. I— It will be good to see you again. And the boys, too."

The gentleness he heard in in her voice was genuine and it caused something in his chest to burgeon with un-explained emotions.

"It will be just as good for me, Stacy," he said huskily. "See you in a bit."

"I'll be watching for you," she said and promptly ended the call.

Win slipped the phone back into his shirt pocket just as Joshua walked up to him.

"Who was on the phone, Dad? You're smiling."

Yeah, he was smiling, Win thought. And it felt good.

"That was Stacy. She's invited us over to the Bonnie B tonight. One of Asa's mares had twins. She thought we might like to see them and have dinner. How does that sound to you?"

Walking up on the tail end of the conversation, Oliver

reacted by making a few fist pumps. "Yay, Dad! Going to the Bonnie B would be awesome!"

Win directed a questioning look at Joshua. "What about you, Joshua? Do you want to go?"

Joshua shrugged both shoulders. "Would it make any difference if I didn't?"

"If you're asking if I'd call Stacy back and tell her we weren't coming, then my answer is no. But I'd like for you to want to go."

Joshua paused for a moment then grinned and nodded. "I'm with Oliver. Seeing twin baby horses would be cool. And I'm kinda starting to like Ms. Abernathy."

Win was beginning to like her, too, he thought. Whether that was good or bad remained to be seen.

An hour later, Stacy was standing on the porch of the ranch house when she spotted Win's black truck coming up the gravel road that ran in front of the house and farther on to the ranch yard.

Unable to contain her excitement, she quickly bound down the steps and across the yard, then passed through the gate to wait for him to bring the truck to a stop.

"Hi, Win!" she called as he stepped down from the cab. "Welcome to the Bonnie B again. I'm so happy you could make it."

"Hi, Stacy!" he greeted. "Thanks for inviting us."

While he reached back into the vehicle for his jacket, Joshua and Oliver climbed from the back seat. Stacy said hello to them both before she turned to see Win shrugging the denim garment over his plaid flannel shirt.

"We hurried to get over here before dark, but I'd forgotten just how far it is from the J Barb to the Bonnie B," he told her. "I hope we're not holding up dinner."

"Not at all. In fact, we still have plenty of time to go see the foals. And no worries about it getting dark. There's plenty of lights in and around the barn," she assured him then turned her attention to the boys. "Are you guys ready to see the new babies?"

"Oh yeah!" Oliver exclaimed. "We've never had a baby horse on our ranch before. I can't wait to see them."

"I'm excited to see them, too," Joshua admitted. "Dad says twin foals are rare."

"He's right. They don't come along very often." She gestured toward a barn to the right of a large hay shed. "They're over in the big barn."

The four of them made their way across a wide expanse of graveled ground until they reached one end of the barn where a door with a wooden latch was located.

"This is actually the back entrance of the barn," she told Win as she lifted the wood handle and opened the door. "But this end of the building is where most of the horses are kept. That is, the horses that Dad wants stalled. The rest of the remuda runs loose in a pasture on the far east end of the ranch yard."

"We only have two horses on the J Barb," Oliver told her. "But Dad says he's gonna get two more pretty soon. That way all three of us will have a horse to ride and one extra in case we need it."

"Sounds like a good plan," Stacy said to him.

Win chuckled. "Especially for a kid who's crazy about horses," he said as he gave Oliver's head an affectionate scrub.

"Me and Oliver can ride good," Joshua told her. "Can you?"

Surprised and pleased that the teenager was making conversation with her, she looked at him and smiled. "Actually, I'm not all that good at horseback riding. I can stay aboard, but I do a lot of bouncing around. My brothers say I'm hopeless as a cowgirl. But my sister, Robin, is good at riding. She knows all about horses."

"My mom could ride good," Joshua said. "Couldn't she, Dad?"

Darting a glance at Win, Stacy expected to see a dark expression on his face. Instead, he gave her a wry smile that said his late wife would always be a part of their lives. The idea would probably discourage some women from trying to have a relationship with Win, but Stacy was trying not to let it daunt her. After all, it wouldn't be normal or respectful for any man to dismiss memories of his late wife, she thought.

"Yes. She was an excellent horsewoman," Win answered his son.

"I bet Ms. Abernathy could be excellent, too," Oliver spoke up. "If she tried hard."

The fact that Oliver wanted to defend her was so sweet, it brought a mist of tears to her eyes. After blinking the moisture away, she looked up at Win and smiled.

"I'd have to quit shaking in my boots first," she joked.

All four of them entered the barn and Stacy carefully latched the door behind them before they started walking down a wide alleyway with horse stalls situated on both sides. Fluorescent lights hung from the rafters and cast a soft glow over the entire interior of the building. Down the center of the high, open ceiling, heaters fastened to an iron I-beam were currently blowing warm air down into the stalls. At the far end of the building, a radio was playing soft music and the sound intermingled with the rustle of hay and the exchange of soft nickers between the horses.

"This is quite a setup," Win said as he gazed curiously

around him. "I'd say the Bonnie B has some pampered horses."

"Dad loves his animals and his children." She slanted him an impish grin. "And you're probably thinking he spoils all of us."

He arched a quizzical brow at her. "Not really. You and your siblings don't appear to be spoiled."

Her grin turned into an all-out smile as she stepped closer to his side and slipped her arm through his. "Thank you, Win. That's one of the nicest things you've said to me."

"Well, it's obvious you and everyone in your family all work for what you have. Besides, money and what it can buy isn't the only way a person can be spoiled."

"You're right. I see it every day with some of my little students."

Joshua and Oliver had walked on ahead of the adults and were now peering into each stall they passed. When they reached the one with the mare and her foals, they both dropped to their knees and peered through the bottom slats of the enclosure to get a better view.

"I told them not to be yelling, so they wouldn't scare the foals or the other horses," Win told her, adding with a chuckle, "I'm actually surprised they're following my orders. I guess they're too enthralled to start shouting."

Smiling up at him, she squeezed his arm. "I'm glad they're excited to see the foals. I wanted them to enjoy this evening. I want you to enjoy it, too."

"You needn't worry about that." He placed a hand over the one she had resting on his arm. "I'm glad you invited us. And the boys will be telling all their friends about this."

They reached the stall where Joshua and Oliver were still engrossed with the matching chestnut-colored foals and, for the next few minutes, all attention was on the mare and her babies.

"Dad named the one with the white star on its forehead Star," Stacy said with a little laugh. "Not very original, but it fits the little fellow. And the one with the white lightning bolt on its forehead has been named Comet. He's the feisty one."

"Star and Comet! Boy, I sure wish we had a pair of baby horses like this," Joshua exclaimed. "They're going to be awesome when they grow up."

"Look how tiny their feet are, Dad!" Oliver noted excitedly. "And they have white on their legs, too."

"Those are called stockings," Joshua informed his brother. "Right, Dad?"

"That's right, son."

A footstep sounded behind them and Stacy turned to see Rueben, one of the Bonnie B's long-time ranch hands, had walked up to them. As soon as Stacy began to introduce the rail-thin man to Win and his sons, he set down the bucket of water he was toting and pushed a battered brown hat back off his forehead to reveal a thick swathe of iron-gray hair.

"Nice to meet you folks," he said, shaking each of their hands.

"Looks like you're bringing fresh water to Lizzy," she said to the older man.

Rueben nodded. "She needs to drink plenty. It's going to take lots of milk to feed these two."

"What if she doesn't have enough milk?" Joshua asked worriedly.

Rueben gave the teenager a toothy grin. "Oh, if that was to happen, we'd bring out the bottle and feed them by hand. Don't you worry, son, these little hosses won't ever go hungry."

"What kind of milk would go in the bottle?" Oliver wanted to know. "Horse milk?"

Chuckling, Rueben winked at Stacy and Win, then began to explain to the boys all about milk formula and the nutrients needed to feed a foal. As they listened intently, Stacy pulled Win to one side.

"Would you like to go for a walk around the ranch yard?" she asked. "I'll tell Rueben to keep an eye on the boys and show them the rest of the stalled horses."

His hand came to rest against the middle of her back as he gave her a clever little smile. "How did you know that was exactly what I wanted to do?"

Her heart beating fast, she flashed him a pointed grin. "Oh, it was just a guess."

After Stacy instructed Rueben to keep a watch on the boys, she and Win walked to the far end of the barn where another door opened out to a long loafing shed.

"When the weather is cold and wet, some of the cattle bunch under here for shelter," she explained. "And there's two more longer loafing sheds than this one out beyond that barn you can see in the distance. Right now, most of our cattle are still on the ranges grazing on what's left of the summer grass. What about yours?"

"I'm going to have to start buying hay soon. But that's to be expected."

He snugged his arm tighter around the back of her waist and urged her away from the barn door. As they walked over to the overhang of the tin roof, she took in a deep breath and said, "I'm going to make a confession, Win. I thought long and hard before I called you. I was afraid you'd think I was being forward and trying to twist your arm just so I—uh, could see you again."

His warm chuckle reassured her that she'd not made a mess of things with him.

"Stacy, you're hardly the forward type. And you're sure not big enough to twist my arm," he teased and then his voice lowered to a husky tone. "I'm glad you called and I'm glad I'm here. And in case you didn't know, you look beautiful tonight."

Laughing softly, she glanced down at her old jeans, simple brown ranch jacket and the yellow muffler she'd tied loosely around her neck. "Not like this. But thank you, anyway."

With his hands on both sides of her waist, he turned her so that she was facing him. "Stacy, I don't think you invited me out here to talk about cattle or hay. And I didn't come out here to talk agriculture or ranching."

Even though they were standing in the shadows, there was just enough light for her to see stark need on his face. The sight of it put a lump in her throat and turned her voice into little more than a whisper.

"No. I guess I need to make a second confession," she said. "I wanted to be alone with you. After the picnic, I—"

The remainder of her words were lost as he let out a low groan and tugged her body forward until it was pressed to his.

"I can't get you and that day out of my mind, Stacy. I've tried. But I keep thinking about you and this."

Even as he said the words, his face was drawing down to hers, making it clear what he meant by *this*.

Closing her eyes, she breathed his name and tilted her lips up to his. The contact of his hard lips was just as magical as she remembered and as he quickly deepened the kiss, a rush of hot pleasure swept over her.

With a tiny moan, she wrapped her arms around his

waist and leaned in against his hard, lean body. Her lips couldn't deny how much she wanted and needed him and she tried to let her kiss convey all the warm and wonderful feelings he evoked in her.

When he finally raised his head enough for them to drag in deep breaths, he reached up and stroked his fingers through the long strands of hair waving away from her forehead. The touch of his big hand was incredibly gentle and she found herself wishing and wanting his hands to touch more than her face or hair. She wanted to have them moving over every part of her body. She wanted to feel his rough palms sliding against her bare skin.

"I don't understand this, Stacy," he mouthed against her cheek. "No matter how much I kiss you, I still want more."

"Yes. Oh yes. I want more, too." She leaned her head back and met his gaze in the semidarkness. "That's why I wanted to see you again—to see if your kisses still turned my senses upside down."

His hands slipped to the middle of her back and tugged her upper body even tighter to his. "Do they?"

A little breathless laugh rushed past her lips and, in the back of her mind, Stacy wondered if she was morphing into a different woman right there in Win's arms. She'd never felt like this with any man. She'd never said such words to any man. And yet, with Win, it all felt natural and right.

"I think you've given them an even harder shake tonight," she murmured.

A lopsided grin twisted his lips. "I can't tell you what you've done to mine. I'm too addled to think."

She reached up and cupped her hand to the side of his face. "I'm a boring little school teacher, Win. I don't know the first thing about addling a man's senses. At least, not a man like you."

The grin on his lips deepened. "What does that mean? A man like me?"

Her cheeks were hot, but she didn't care if he could see she was blushing. The longer she was in his arms, the more her inhibitions slipped off into the darkness.

"You're not a geek, like most of my dates have been. And I'm not a sexy siren."

One of his hands moved to the back of her head and, as his fingers meshed in her hair, she felt certain she was going to melt right there in his arms.

"You underestimate yourself, Stacy. You're sexy as hell to me."

He didn't wait for her to respond with words. He lowered his head back to hers and this time when his lips fastened roughly over hers, she opened her mouth and invited his tongue to plunge inside.

Somewhere beyond the loud roar in her ears, she heard his needy groan, and somewhere in the far distance, a cow answered the bawl of her calf. Closer to the house, the engine of a vehicle fired to life, while just beyond the loafing shed where they stood, she could hear the wind rattling the leaves on the cottonwood tree. Strange that all those sounds could penetrate her senses even while she was enraptured by the taste of him, the warmth of his body enveloping hers, and the fire igniting each kiss.

A glorious obsession.

Yes, she thought. That described her feelings for Win perfectly.

Their embrace must have gone on for much longer than Stacy knew. By the time he finally pulled away from her, she was practically limp with the need for oxygen and she had to clutch his forearms to steady herself.

"Stacy, I—*we* need to get back to the barn. Before the boys come looking for us."

Gulping in a deep breath, she nodded. "You're right. We, uh, have probably been out here longer than I thought."

"We didn't get very far on our tour of the ranch yard," he said.

Her short laugh was more like a cough. "No. We sort of got sidetracked. Next time you're here, I'll show you the ranch yard for real."

His hand came to rest on her shoulder and she glanced up to see an uncertain expression on his face. She didn't know what he was thinking, but whatever was on his mind, she was bound and determined to deal with it.

"Next time? Is there going to be a next time?" he asked.

"Certainly. Why wouldn't there be?"

He took a moment, as if considering his response. "I don't know, Stacy. I—I'm not sure I'm ready for this. Something happens when the two of us get together. It's…"

"Deep? And a little scary?" she finished for him.

With a helpless groan, he buried his face in the side of her hair. "To me, it's a whole lot scary."

She turned her head just enough to rub her cheek against his. "This is all new for me, Win. Since I met you, my life has started to change, and I guess that's a little frightening. But it's a wonderful kind of frightening. Kind of like an adventure you've always wanted to take into the wilderness, but you're not sure what's waiting for you once you get to your destination. You just have to trust everything will be good."

He pulled his head back and she could see an anguished frown twisting his features. "That sounds very optimistic, Stacy. Or maybe I should say courageous."

She didn't let his doubtful expression get her down. He'd

just made love to her with his kisses and, for now, that was enough to lend her all the hope she needed.

"That's better than being a doom and gloom person. Something I'm guilty of being too many times. I don't want to view myself or the future in that way. I want to be optimistic and I want the same thing for you."

His features softened and, for a moment, Stacy thought he might kiss her again, but then his arm came around her shoulders and turned her toward the barn door.

"We'd better go in," he said. "Before the boys start missing us. And I decide to kiss you again."

Chapter Eight

A few minutes later, when Bonnie announced dinner was ready, Win was surprised that more of the Abernathy family hadn't showed up to partake of the evening meal. This time, with only Stacy and her parents, and Win and his boys seated at the table, the meal felt much more intimate. Especially with Stacy sitting at his side.

Win couldn't deny the closeness he felt to Stacy, or the warm pleasure her presence gave him. He even caught himself wondering if their lives would always be this idyllic if they were to deepen their relationship and become man and wife. He'd have a whole family again and his sons would have a mother. But nothing remained perfect and blissful. Yvette's sudden death had opened his eyes to that dismal fact. And yet, when Stacy looked at him with her soft blue eyes or touched her hand to his, he wanted to believe things could be different with her. He wanted to think he had the right to have as much happiness as the next person.

"Grandpa Doyle has eight horses on the Jackson Ranch. But he doesn't have any baby horses."

Oliver's comment pulled Win out of his wandering thoughts and he glanced across the table to see Asa listening intently to the boy's conversation.

"Do you ride your grandfather's horses when you visit your grandparents' ranch?" Asa asked him.

"Oh yeah, me and Joshua ride with him to check on the cows. He has a great big herd of Black Baldies like ours," Oliver told him.

"Does your grandmother help with the ranch work?" Bonnie asked, her smile encompassing both boys. "Or is she more like me—the cook of the crew?"

"Oh, Grandma Audrey does chores around the ranch yard. Like feeding the dogs and cats and sometimes the horses. And she cooks, too," Oliver answered. "Mostly things like stew or beans."

"She makes blueberry pies all the time," Joshua added. "Because that's Grandpa's favorite. That and apple. My mom made huckleberry pies. 'Cause we had a ton of huckleberry bushes on our ranch, didn't we, Dad?"

Win glanced down the table to where Joshua was sitting next to his younger brother. He was somewhat surprised at how much his sons appeared to be enjoying their talk with Stacy's parents. But with the older couple having five kids of their own, plus grandchildren, they seemed to know exactly how to communicate with Joshua and Oliver.

"Yes. Until a mountain fire swept through and burned most of them," Win replied. "After that, the berries were few and far between."

Joshua nodded as he swallowed a bite of enchilada. "Yeah. I remember Mom cried about the berries burning up."

Oliver looked wistfully at his brother. "I wish I could remember her like you do. I only get to look at her picture. She was real pretty. She had brown hair and a smile like she was happy."

Joshua frowned at him. "That's because Mom was

happy. And Dad was happy. And so was I. But then she died." He turned a bleak expression on Asa and Bonnie. "Back then, I didn't know anyone as young as Mom could die. I thought that only happened to old people. But I guess it can happen to anybody. Even me or Oliver."

Asa and Bonnie were giving both boys empathetic looks while, beneath the table, Stacy reached over and gently rested her hand on Win's thigh as if to tell him she understood how hard it was for him to hear his sons talk about their mother's sudden death. The fact that Stacy was so sensitive to his and his sons feelings, and how genuinely empathetic she was to the whole situation, touched Win deeply.

Asa said, "That much is true, Joshua. But dying isn't something a person should dwell on. Otherwise, he'll ruin the time he's living. Do you understand what I'm trying to say?"

After giving the man's words a long thought, Joshua nodded. "Yeah. It means we shouldn't worry about what happened a long time ago. We should think about now and all the fun we're gonna have later on."

Asa gave the teenager a nod of approval. "You're right on target, Joshua."

Oliver looked around the table at the adults. "I used to get really scared when Joshua talked about our mom dying," he admitted. "I thought if it happened to her, it might happen to me. I told Grandpa Doyle what I was thinking and he told me that's not the way things worked. After that, I'm not a scaredy-cat anymore."

Bonnie looked over at Win and winked. "You have two very smart sons, Win. You should be proud."

I'm not a scaredy-cat anymore. Oh, God, Win hadn't known his little Oliver had been so afraid because his mother had died. He'd not really understood the confusion

Joshua had felt over Yvette's sudden death. They'd never really talked about their fears to Win and he'd thought they were coping okay with the loss. Now, listening to them express their feelings to the Abernathys, he hated himself for not digging deeper into his sons' thoughts, because clearly Yvette's death had taken a psychological toll on his sons. Oh, he'd understood it wasn't easy for them to be without their mother. But he'd told himself that as long as they weren't crying or moping about, they were dealing with the void in their lives.

Win reached for his water glass and took a drink before he replied, "I am, Bonnie. Very proud."

"I think Win's sons aren't just smart, they're hungry, too," Asa told his wife. "Pass those boys some more enchiladas. I'll bet they can eat a second plateful."

"Can I have rice and beans, too?" Oliver asked Asa.

Win let out a good-natured groan, while everyone else at the table laughed.

"Sure, you can," Bonnie told Oliver. "But you need to save room for dessert. We're having tres leches cake."

"What's that?"

The question was spoken in unison by both boys, and as Bonnie began to describe the milk-soaked cake, Win leaned his head toward Stacy and spoke in a low voice. "My sons are enjoying the heck out of this meal, but what is it doing to your parents?" he asked.

She slanted him a coy smile. "Trust me. They're loving every minute of it. And in case you're wondering, so am I."

Win didn't want to be thrilled by her words. He didn't want to remember the delicious heat of her kisses or to think about making love to her. But he was. And there didn't seem to be a thing he could do about it.

Once dinner was over, Win stayed long enough to have

coffee in the den with Stacy and her parents before he announced it was time for him and the boys to head home to the J Barb.

As Joshua and Oliver fetched their coats from a hall closet, Stacy joined Win on the front porch while he waited for the children.

"I wish it wasn't a school night," she said. "Joshua and Oliver would've enjoyed making another trip to the barn to see Comet and Star before you left."

Win would've enjoyed another trip himself. That was exactly why it was a good thing it was time for him and the boys to go home. Otherwise, he'd be greatly tempted to carry her off to some shadowy spot and make love to her.

"They would definitely like seeing the babies again. But by the time I get them home and to bed, it's going to be getting late."

She reached for his hand and he gladly wrapped his fingers around hers.

"You're right," she said. "It's just that I wish we had more time together. This evening has been so nice."

Nice was too meek a word to describe what this night had been for him. He'd had his eyes opened to his children and to Stacy. She wasn't just a pretty girl with a warm smile. She was a woman who fit perfectly in his arms and, with each minute that passed, she was growing ever dearer to him.

His fingers gently smoothed over the back of her hand. "Yes, it has."

Her gaze on his, Win could see doubt flickering in her eyes. The sight of it surprised him. Hadn't his kisses told her how much he'd enjoyed being with her?

"Do you really mean that?" she asked.

"Yes, I do. Why would you think otherwise?"

She shrugged and glanced away from him. "Oh. Sometimes it feels like you're somewhere far away and not with me."

Sometimes he was far away, Win realized. He was revisiting that place and time in his mind and heart when he'd been happy and a moment later his world had gone dark.

"I'm not far away from you. I'm just thinking." He gave her a rueful smile. "My mother used to say I lived in my head too much. I guess I'm still guilty of that."

She started to reply but at that moment the front door of the house opened and Joshua and Oliver stepped onto the porch.

"Look, Dad! Bonnie gave us a box of cowboy cookies to take home with us!" Oliver held up the small cardboard box for his father to see. "Wasn't that nice of her?"

"I hope you thanked her for the gift," Win said.

"We both thanked her, Dad." Joshua spoke up. "And she said to tell you that she put a couple of extra cookies in there for you."

Stacy laughed at the helpless look on Win's face. "Mom doesn't limit her spoiling to only children. You might as well get used to it."

Oh yes, Win mused. He could get used to all of this family togetherness and having thoughtful things done for him. But would he ever get past the fear of losing it? And her?

Shoving the troubling thought out of his mind, he motioned for the boys to go to the truck and, as they bounded down the steps and trotted across the yard, Win and Stacy followed in a slow walk.

Throughout the short trek to the truck, neither of them spoke one word. However, when they reached the driver's door, Win felt compelled to bring up the subject of seeing her again.

"I'd like for us to get together sometime soon," he said. "Would you?"

"I'd like that very much."

The soft smile on her face caused his stomach to take a funny little tumble. "Well, my schedule is always changing. I promised three different students I'd stop by their homes after school to look over their show animals. And Joshua has decided to go out for basketball, so I'll be staying over late in the evenings to pick him up from practice."

Her smile deepened as if to say she wasn't a bit deterred. "I understand. You're not only a teacher, you're also a father. That makes you have double duty," she told him. "Well, maybe we can get together on the weekend. I'll certainly be free."

"Okay. I— Uh, I'll call you." Bending his head, he pressed a kiss to her cheek. "Good night, Stacy."

"Good night," she murmured.

Win quickly climbed into the truck and as he put the vehicle into forward motion, she stepped back and gave him a little wave.

Win waved back then, pressing on the accelerator, he determinedly focused on the dark road ahead of him.

"Dad, did I see you kiss Ms. Abernathy on the cheek?" Joshua asked.

"Yes. You did."

"Wow!" Oliver exclaimed. "Does that mean you like her a whole lot?"

A strange fullness suddenly settled in the middle of Win's chest.

"Yes. I like her a whole lot."

Win expected to hear some loud responses to his answer. Instead, long moments passed with both boys being unusually quiet. It wasn't until he'd turned off the gravel road on the Bonnie B and onto the highway that he heard his sons whispering back and forth to each other.

No doubt the boys were discussing their father's interest in a woman and wondering if this relationship would cause as much upheaval as the one he'd had with Tara.

"Don't worry, boys. Nothing is going to make us move from Bronco. I can promise you that," he said firmly.

Oliver leaned forward. "Oh, we're not worried, Dad. Are we, Joshua?"

"We're not worried about that or anything," Joshua declared.

Great, Win sheepishly muttered to himself. His ten- and fifteen-year-old sons had more confidence about the future than he did.

When the weekend arrived, Stacy was definitely expecting to hear from Win and she spent both days eagerly waiting for her phone to ring with his call, or at the very least, to signal her with a text message. Surely, he wanted to keep in touch and let her know about his schedule. But Saturday and Sunday both passed without a word from him and, by the middle of the following week with still no call or message, she had to face the fact that he'd changed his mind about seeing her again. Or perhaps he'd never intended to call her in the first place.

The idea hurt her more than she wanted to admit and, for the past couple of days, she'd begun to ask herself if she was making a mistake in trying to have a relationship with the guy. He'd been single for more than seven years. He didn't want a woman in his life on a permanent basis. That much was clear. And yet she'd felt more than just desire in his kiss. She'd felt loneliness and need and a reluctance to let her go.

"You're not eating your lunch, Stacy. Are you sick?"

The question came from Emma, who was sitting next to Stacy at a table near the back of the school cafeteria.

Stacy looked down to see she'd eaten only a small portion of the grilled chicken and vegetables on her plate. "I'm not very hungry today. I should've just gotten a carton of milk and left off the food."

Emma snorted. "You can't go all day on a carton of milk. And you don't have an extra pound to lose."

She deliberately stabbed her fork into a chunk of chicken and popped it into her mouth, but for all she knew, it could have been a lump of wet cardboard. "I'm not trying to lose weight," she said more crossly than she intended. "I just don't have an appetite today."

"Sorry. I wasn't scolding you," Emma said. "I'm concerned about you, that's all."

Stacy looked out over the rows of tables where the first- and second-grade students were busy eating. Up to this point of the lunch break, the children had been behaved, which was a relief. Normally, it didn't ruffle her nerves if she had to deal with loud arguments or rowdiness during the midday meal, but today she was rattled.

Sighing, she looked regrettably at her friend and co-worker. "No, I'm the one who's sorry, Emma. I didn't mean to sound sharp. I'm...well, I'm having a hard time today."

Emma shook her head. "I think you've been having a hard time all week. I didn't want to mention it to you, but you've not been yourself."

Groaning, Stacy placed her fork on the side of her plate. "I feel worse than stupid, Emma. I think I've made a big fool of myself and it hurts."

Emma's expression turned grim. "Does this have anything to do with Win Jackson?"

Heaving out a heavy breath, Stacy nodded. "I mistakenly thought he was becoming interested in me. Seriously interested. I couldn't have been more wrong."

"What happened? He told you to keep your distance? That he had other fish to fry?"

Stacy glanced down at her wrap dress. With bright orange and yellow swirls running through the fabric, it was one of her favorite fall garments and she'd purposely worn the dress today in the hope it would boost her spirits. Instead, she was wondering why she'd bothered.

"No. Nothing like that. He and the boys visited the ranch last week and had dinner with us. The evening was…well, very nice. He even said so himself."

"That all sounds great to me. So what's making the corners of your mouth droop?" Emma wanted to know.

Feeling a bit juvenile, Stacy picked up her fork and stabbed another chunk of chicken. "He promised to call— to let me know when we could get together again. And he hasn't. That was a week ago. It's obvious that what little interest he had in me has fizzled completely."

Emma dipped a spoon into a chocolate pudding cup. "Maybe his phone is broken. Or he's been too busy."

Stacy snorted. "Joshua has a phone he could borrow. As for being busy, how long does it take to send a short text message?" She rolled her eyes helplessly toward the ceiling. "I guess it's pretty obvious that, where men are concerned, I'm naive. But I truly thought Win was different."

"Hmm. He is different, Stacy. He's a widower and he's been single for a long time. If you want my honest opinion, he's probably having second thoughts about getting involved with you. But that's not to say he's writing you off. He just needs time."

Stacy frowned. "Seven years isn't enough?"

"Grief can't be measured with time, Stacy." She leveled a pointed look at her. "But forget all of that. If you're that concerned, call him."

Stacy didn't want to admit that the only reason Win'd had dinner on the Bonnie B last Wednesday night was that she'd taken it upon herself to invite him. But she had no intentions of doing the inviting a second time. She might be a fool, but she wasn't a man chaser.

"I get what you're saying, Emma. But for now, I don't think that's the right thing for me to do."

Emma shook her head and sighed. "Well, it's your life and your business. And considering my track record with love and marriage, I'm hardly one to be handing out advice."

Realizing the bright sunshine that had been slanting across their table had disappeared, Stacy glanced over at the row of windows that overlooked the playground. Rain had started to fall and she thought how much the weather matched her somber mood.

"Look, Emma. We can forget about having outside recess this afternoon."

Emma glanced at the rain beating against the windowpanes and chuckled. "All in a day's work, my dear," she said then reached over and gave Stacy's forearm an encouraging pat. "Cheer up. You're going to see sunshine again. Probably sooner than you think."

Stacy wasn't one to give up. Especially on something she believed to be worthwhile. But it was becoming more and more difficult to think Win could ever fall in love with her.

Later that night as Win sat at the kitchen table, grading a stack of test papers, he wondered if it was the rain making the house seem unusually dark and chilly. The lights were burning over the table and the stove located a few feet away. The furnace was blowing warm air through the vents on floor. Why did he feel like he was sitting in a cold tomb?

Don't play ignorant, Win. The house has nothing to do with the chill you're feeling and everything to do with Stacy. You need her. You just don't want to admit it.

Tossing his red pencil onto the pile of papers, he scrubbed his face with both hands. He felt awful about not calling her. Especially when he'd told her he would. But not following through on his word was only one of the reasons he was feeling miserable. No matter how hard he tried to ignore it or to deny it, he was aching to see her again.

For a week now, he'd fought with himself over this emotional tangle he'd gotten into with Stacy. She brought so many wonderful things to his life, yet the wounded part of him couldn't forget all the things that could go wrong.

Muttering a frustrated oath, he left his chair to pour a cup of coffee from the carafe sitting on the cabinet. Once he'd stirred in a spoonful of sugar, he glanced at the clock above the refrigerator.

It was late enough for the boys to already be in bed, but not so late that his brother back in Whitehorn would be asleep. Maybe if he could hear Shawn's voice, he could lift himself out of this dismal pit he'd fallen into.

Back at the table, he picked up his cell phone and carried it and his coffee out to the living room to take a seat in an armchair that overlooked a large picture window. At the moment, the only thing he could see in the glow of the yard lamp was sheets of rain pounding against the west end of the barn.

Shawn answered on the third ring and Win could tell by the groggy sound of his voice that he'd been dozing.

"Sorry, brother. Have you already gone to bed?"

"No. I've been watching something very exciting on TV. Can't you tell?"

Win smiled in spite of himself. "Yeah. So exciting, you dozed off."

"I'm guilty." He paused long enough to yawn then said, "But I have a good excuse. The episode was a rerun."

"Okay. So you're not entering old age yet."

"Not yet. What are you doing up this late anyway?" Shawn asked. "Has something happened?"

"No. I'm grading test papers," Win told him. "Your nephews are snug in bed. It's pouring rain here, and cold, and I was just sort of feeling lonely."

The was a silent pause and then Shawn asked, "Are you wishing you were back in Whitehorn?"

Was he? Funny how these past few days that thought had never entered his mind. "Hell no!"

"That was plain enough."

Win grimaced. "Don't get me wrong. I love seeing you and Mom and Dad. But otherwise, I don't miss it. Bronco is suiting me and the boys just fine."

"I'm glad to hear it. So why are you feeling lonely?"

Win closed his eyes and pressed his fingers against the burning lids. "I shouldn't have said lonely, Shawn. That's not really how I'm feeling. I'm messed up—in my head or my heart—I don't know which. Except that I'm miserable."

"Don't tell me. You've met a woman. Not only met her, but you've fallen for her."

Shawn was so close to the truth that Win's eyes popped open and he sat straight up in the chair. "Sometimes you make me sick."

Shawn laughed. "Why? Because I'm clairvoyant? Or because I'm your annoying little brother?"

With a good-natured groan, Win said, "Both, I suppose.

But you're right, as usual. I have met a woman and I… I'm not ready to say I've fallen for her, but I—"

"You're so close to falling that you're on the verge of teetering off the cliff," Shawn finished for him.

"Yeah. And I'm scared to death."

"Why? You believe if you don't give her an engagement ring, she'll set off on a vendetta to ruin you? Like Tara went after you?" He snorted in Win's ear. "I can't imagine any woman being as vengeful as her. Unless it was my ex."

Win sipped his coffee before he answered. "Actually, I'm not thinking anything like that. Stacy is not that kind of a person. She looks at things reasonably and open-mindedly. She wouldn't hurt a fly. Unless it was biting her and, even then, she'd probably gently brush it away instead of smashing it with a swatter."

"The soft, gentle kind, huh? Nothing wrong with that. I always thought I wanted the strong, independent type. You know, a woman who could take care of herself instead of smothering me. Look how wrong I was."

"Vicki wasn't strong and independent. She was a cheater and a liar. There's a huge difference."

Shawn let out a heavy sigh. "I believe I'm supposed to live my life as a single man, Win. But not you. You were a great husband to Yvette and you're the best of fathers. It's in the cards for you to find love again."

Love. Ever since Win had met Stacy, he'd been shying away from that word. He'd not wanted to consider how it would be to love her. He'd not wanted to imagine how his life would be to have her by his side, loving him, support-ing him. But now he could think of little else.

"You don't have a crystal ball, little brother. And neither do I, but I am certain about one thing. The more I'm with Stacy, the more I want to be with her. And—"

Shawn interjected, "Just how well do you know this woman? Stacy is her name?"

"Yes. Stacy Abernathy. There are several branches of the Abernathys around Bronco. From what I understand, it's an old, monied name—at the top tier of Bronco society. As for Stacy's branch of the family, they are definitely well off. One look at their ranch, the Bonnie B, and you know they're not hurting financially. But I can truly say they're not snobs."

"Hmm. So Stacy is an heiress. That's interesting."

Win grunted as he leaned over and placed his cup on a low table positioned next to his chair. "Being an heiress is the least interesting thing about her. She teaches second grade at Bronco Elementary, where Oliver goes to school. Besides being a dedicated teacher, she's beautiful and sweet, and is very good with children. I should probably also mention she's twenty-eight and never been engaged or married."

After a short pause, Shawn said, "I'm really curious now, Win. With this kind of résumé, why are you second-guessing getting involved with the woman? She sounds perfect for you."

Groaning, Win wearily pinched the bridge of his nose. "That's just it, Shawn. Perfection doesn't last. I…uh, don't think I could survive having my family shattered a second time."

Silence stretched again before Shawn finally spoke. "Hmm. You're thinking she won't stick with you? Or you have the morbid idea that she'll die from some medical problem or get killed in an accident?"

Hearing Shawn speaking Win's fears out loud made it all sound ridiculous. Even worse, it made Win appear as a coward.

Which you are, Win. Don't ever take your shirt off in

front of Stacy. Unless you want her to see the giant yellow streak down your back.

Silently cursing at the taunting voice in his head, he said to Shawn, "Okay, I'll admit it. When I think of getting into a serious relationship with Stacy, all kinds of tragedies enter my mind. Call me stupid, but I just can't help it."

"All I can say is, you'd better give yourself a hard mental slap, brother. Otherwise, you're going to be worse than lonely. You're going to be downright miserable. I—"

Win interrupted his brother before he could say more. "Shawn, all of this is easy for you to say when it was *my* wife that died! You don't know what it feels like, or what it's done to me!"

"You're right, I can't understand what it feels like to have a spouse die. But I can plainly see what Yvette's death has done to you, and it's not good. When are you going to open your eyes and realize that you're not the only widower in this world? That you can't hang on to her ghost forever?"

Was he hanging on to Yvette's ghost? He'd never imagined himself doing such a thing. The only photos of Yvette that were sitting out in clear view were in Joshua's and Oliver's bedrooms. He'd purposely kept all reminders of her from the remaining rooms of the house. And he could truthfully say there were days that his late wife never entered his mind.

"You don't know what you're talking about, Shawn," he said flatly. "I'm not hanging on to Yvette's ghost."

"Maybe not her exactly, but you're hanging on to losing her. That's just as debilitating."

Win wanted to argue the point but deep down he realized that Shawn was right. He just didn't want to admit the truth, or to face it.

Closing his eyes, Win rested his head against the back

of the armchair. "Okay. So what you're saying is that I need to get a backbone."

"More or less. And I'm saying if you feel anything at all for Stacy, then you need to make yourself clear to her. Instead of sitting back and worrying about all the bad things that could happen. 'Cause life isn't all bad, Win."

"You're right, Shawn. I'm my own worst enemy," Win told him. "Actually, a friend of mine here in Bronco, a coach at the high school, in fact, has basically told me the same thing as you. But hearing it from you has hit me harder."

"Good. I hope everything I've said has hit you over the head," Shawn said with a chuckle. "Remember when we were kids and were always wrestling and punching each other? Back then, I could knock some sense into you. Nowadays I have to do it with words."

Win chuckled along with his brother. "Good thing. I'd hate to have to explain to my students why I had two black eyes."

Shawn laughed and then Win inquired about their parents.

"They're both fine. They miss you and their grandsons. But they're glad you're happy there in Bronco. I won't tell them you've been sitting in a dark room moping over what to do about a woman. There are some things they don't need to know."

No, Win thought. Their parents didn't need to hear that he was still stuck in the same old rut he'd been in since Yvette had died. He wanted his mother and father to think of him as an emotionally strong man.

Wiping a hand over his face, he muttered, "How do you know I'm sitting in a dark room? This isn't a FaceTime call."

Shawn's grunt held a bit of humor. "Remember, I see things even when I don't see them with my eyes. And I'll tell you what I'm seeing right now. You hanging up and calling your pretty teacher."

Call Stacy? He'd let a whole week slip by without saying a word to her. He'd been behaving like a jerk and whatever she was thinking about him now couldn't be good.

"I'm not sure she'd want to hear from me," Win mumbled.

"You won't know unless you try."

In spite of the pouring rain, Win felt his spirits suddenly lift. "You're right, Shawn. So, good night. I'll talk to you later."

He could hear Shawn's smug guffaw as he ended the phone connection.

Already dressed in her pajamas, Stacy was sitting on the side of the bed, running a brush through her long hair, when the cellphone lying on the nightstand rang.

Thinking it was probably a spam call or a wrong number, she took her time laying the brush aside and reaching for the phone. By the time she picked it up, the fourth ring had stopped and she expected to find the caller had hung up.

And then she saw *his* name. She'd given up on hearing from Win and now for him to be calling at such a late hour, she could only think something had happened to him or one of the boys.

Her hand shook as she punched the accept button and moved the phone to her ear. "Hello, Win."

"Hello, Stacy. I realize it's late. Have I caught you at a bad time?"

She frowned as all kinds of anxious thoughts raced through her mind. "No. I can talk. Is anything wrong? Has something happened to Oliver or Joshua?"

"No. They're fine. They were both in bed an hour ago."

He dragged in a deep breath then blew it out. "I—uh, I'm sorry I haven't called sooner. Every day I picked up the phone, but—"

Her lips pressed together. "You got cold feet. Is that what you're trying to say?"

There was a pause and then he said, "Yes. Something like that. I— I've been trying to convince myself that you need someone else in your life. A man who doesn't have all the baggage I'm carrying around. One that can give you all the things you've hoped and planned for."

Her heart winced and she gripped the phone as though it was a lifeline. "Have you managed to convince yourself that you're wrong for me?"

"No. I've come to realize that I need to see you. And I hope you'd like to see me. That is…if you aren't too angry with me."

She was probably being a fool, but Stacy's heart was suddenly singing like a bird in springtime. "I've not been angry with you, Win. Disappointed, but not angry."

He responded with a sound crossed between a groan and a gurgle.

"I don't deserve you, Stacy. In fact, I don't know why you put up with me at all."

Even though she was yet to learn why he'd called, the fact that he hadn't given up on her completely had her heart thumping with hope. "Probably because I think you're worth the trouble," she said, trying to inject a teasing note into her voice.

There was a long pause before he spoke and when he finally did, a pent-up breath rushed out of her.

"Well, I'm hoping you think I'm worth going out to dinner with."

Stunned, she stared at the toes of her fuzzy house shoes without really seeing them. "You mean, like a real date?"

He chuckled, and so did she, and suddenly the cold, rainy night felt like a tropical paradise to Stacy.

"Yes. A real date," he said. "No trips to the barn or stepping around cow chips."

Lowering her voice to a provocative murmur, she said, "For your information, I don't have anything against a trip to the barn—with you."

He chuckled again. "I'll remember that," he said huskily before clearing his throat. "Is there a special restaurant you like? It doesn't have to be in Bronco. If you prefer, we can drive somewhere out of town."

"I'm not particular, Win. You choose and surprise me."

"Okay. Are you free Saturday night? I'd say Friday, but Anthony has a ballgame that evening and he'll be watching the boys for me."

Stacy felt as if she was going to float off the bed and fly around the room. But she did her best to hide the rush of excitement from her voice. She feared if he guessed how giddy he was making her, it might put him off the date completely.

"Saturday night is perfect. I can meet you in town, if it would make things easier for you."

"No way. This is going to be a real date. I'll pick you up at your parents' house on the Bonnie B at six thirty. Is that time okay with you?"

"I'll be ready," she told him. "And, Win, I'm very glad you called."

"I'm very glad I called, too. Good night, Stacy. See you Saturday."

"Yes. Good night."

Once the connection ended, Stacy placed the phone back on the nightstand, then smiled to herself.

Win had asked her on a date! A real date! She didn't know what had motivated him to call or why he'd decided he wanted to see her again. And tonight, she didn't care. Win wanted to be with her and that was the only thing that mattered.

Chapter Nine

On Saturday evening, shortly after six o'clock, Stacy stood in front of the floor-length mirror on her closet door and peered critically at her image. This morning when Win had called to confirm their date, he'd not told her exactly where they'd be dining, he'd only said it was upscale, where they could drink wine in a cozy little corner.

The news that he'd be taking her to a fancy restaurant hadn't surprised her. He'd already hinted he wanted them to go somewhere nice. What had surprised her was the mention of the wine and the cozy corner. For as long as she'd known Win, he hadn't exactly come across as a man who was particularly romantic. Desirable, wildly handsome and very sexy. Yes, yes and yes, he was definitely all those things. But a flower-giving, gaze-at-the-moon type of man? No. But just in case he surprised her, she wanted to look the romantic part.

Now as she studied her midnight-blue dress, she wondered if she'd gone a bit too far with the romantic image. The velvet fabric made the dress look ultra-expensive and the sweetheart neckline was just low enough to show a shadow of cleavage. Teardrop-shaped pearls accented with blue sapphires dangled from her ears, while a matching necklace nestled in the hollow at the base of her throat.

She'd swept the top half of her blond hair up and fastened it with a pearl-adorned clasp to allow the deep waves to cascade down to her back. Her feet were probably going to get cold in the strappy black high heels she'd chosen, but surely she could bear the discomfort for one evening.

Satisfied that she didn't look like she was going to teach a class of second graders, she turned away from the mirror and walked over to the dresser where her hairbrush was lying next to a digital alarm clock. As she picked up the brush, she glanced at the glaring red numbers. Six-fifty. Win was already twenty minutes late, but that was hardly enough to worry her. With two kids and a barn full of animals to see after, he had reason to run behind schedule. And she'd already learned he was usually late in picking up Oliver from school. It had to be an ag teacher thing, she thought.

While she was waiting, she brushed through her hair a second time, tidied up her room and laid out her coat and handbag. By the time she finished those tasks, another ten minutes had passed without a sign of Win.

When the clock eventually rolled to a quarter past seven with still no word from Win, she was beginning to fear he might be going to stand her up completely. But why would he? This morning when he'd called, he'd sounded enthused about their plans.

Deciding it was stupid to keep worrying and wondering, she picked up her phone to call him. However, before she could tap in his number, her phone dinged with an incoming text message.

I've had trouble. Be there in a few minutes.

He'd not bothered to explain the kind of trouble he'd encountered, but that scarcely mattered to Stacy. Win was on his way.

After dropping her phone into her handbag, she snatched it and her coat from the bed and hurried out of her bedroom. She was walking through the living room on her way to the porch when she met Robin entering the front door.

"Oooeee! Look at my little sister!" She hurried over to Stacy and holding on to both her hands, stood back and gave her appearance a keen perusal. "Where are you off to? Someone's wedding? Why wasn't I invited?"

Stacy laughed. "No wedding. And you weren't invited because I'm going on a date—with Win."

Robin's jaw dropped. "Win? Really? When did this happen?"

"He phoned me Wednesday night. I was going to tell you about it, but you've been busy and I have, too." She gave her sister a dreamy smile. "I don't want to…well, put too much into this, but I'm sure you can tell I'm feeling on top of the world."

Gently patting her cheek, Robin said, "Your smile tells me how happy you are. I'm glad, sissy. I hope this is the beginning of everything you've ever wanted."

"I hope so, too." Stacy gave her sister a grateful hug and glanced toward the door as the sound of a vehicle caught her attention. "That's probably him. He's running late, so I'm going out to meet him."

Robin kissed her cheek. "Have a good time."

"I plan to," Stacy said as she hurried through the door.

Win was out of his truck and halfway to the yard gate when he spotted Stacy walking down the porch steps to meet him. Even in the dim light of the yard lamp, he could see she was wearing a lovely dress and a pair of high heels, all of which shouted she was expecting their dinner to be special. He could also see that she looked incredibly beautiful and, the closer she got to him, the faster his heart thumped.

"Hi, Win. I'm so happy to see you finally made it."

For once Win didn't care if any of her family was watching, he pulled her into his arms and placed a brief kiss on her lips. "Stacy, I'm so sorry about being late. I've had a heck of a time getting here."

"What happened?"

Taking her by the hand, he urged her toward the truck. "I'll tell you about it as soon as we get on our way."

After helping her into the cab, he took his place in the driver's seat and quickly steered the truck back in the direction of town.

"I was beginning to think you'd changed your mind and weren't coming." She removed her coat and placed it across her lap before she buckled her seatbelt.

Sighing, he shook his head. "Not a chance. I had tire trouble. After I dropped off the boys at Anthony's house, I'd gotten about five miles out of town when my tire went instantly flat."

"Oh no. A blowout?"

He shook his head. "No. I think I ran over some sort of debris. Anyway, it cut a huge hole in the tire."

"But you had a spare, surely."

Chuckling at her practical remark, he slanted a wry look in her direction. "Yes. I never go anywhere without a spare. But something went haywire with the jack. It wouldn't lift the truck. I worked on the jack for at least twenty minutes and still couldn't get it to work. Finally, I gave up and called Anthony and had him bring his jack out to where I was stranded on the side of the highway."

"You mean no one stopped to offer help?" she asked with

dismay. "Usually, a good Samaritan will show up to lend a hand."

"No such luck tonight." He shook his head. "Anyway, I finally got the tire replaced, but by then I was so dirty and greasy I had to turn around and go back to the J Barb to change clothes." He shot her an apologetic look. "I really hate that all this happened, Stacy. I wanted this date to be special."

A relieved breath rushed out of her. He hadn't called to cancel their outing and that was all that mattered. "Don't worry about it, Win," she told him. "Just being with you will make it special."

His groan was full of misgivings. "I'm glad you think so, because it's an hour's drive from Bronco to the restaurant where I had made reservations and there's no way we can make it on time. I had to call and cancel, so I hope you won't mind eating elsewhere. We could try to get reservations at DJ's Deluxe, but it's Saturday night. At this hour I doubt we'd have much luck."

"Right. And I'm too hungry to sit around and wait for a table to become empty there or anywhere else." She flashed him a cheery smile. "Let's find a place where we can just walk in and sit down."

Win allowed his gaze to leave the road long enough to take a brief survey of the dark blue dress clinging to her curves and the way the top part of her hair was pulled up to cascade in shiny waves against her back. This wasn't the same woman he'd first met at the elementary school, or the one who'd escorted him through the horse barn on the Bonnie B. This Stacy looked so alluring and sexy; she was making every masculine cell in his body stand at attention.

Turning his focus back on his driving, he said, "Fine

with me. But you look so beautiful tonight, Stacy. You're fit for a queen's ballroom and I've messed up everything."

"Nonsense. I rarely have a reason to dress up and you gave me one. I'm thankful to you for that much."

He glanced ruefully down at his jeans and dark green shirt. "You probably won't believe this, but I did dress up more than usual this evening. But rolling around beneath the truck trying to fix that damned tire left me looking like a mechanic. But don't worry, at least I have a jacket in the back seat and can cover up most of this wrinkled shirt."

She shook her head. "You look fine, Win. You look better than fine. You look exactly like the man I want to be with. And as for our dinner, I'm sure we'll find something yummy."

"Thanks for being so patient," he told her.

She slanted him a wry smile. "You have to remember I'm a second-grade teacher. My middle name is Patience."

He cocked a curious brow at her. "Is it really Patience?"

"No. But it should be," she said with a soft laugh. "Anyway, I'm sure teaching teenagers all these years has taught you to be laid-back and easygoing."

A short laugh burst out of him. "I'm glad you weren't with me earlier this evening when the jack wouldn't work."

She chuckled. "Well, you are human. And we all have our moments."

"What did Joshua and Oliver think about you going on a date?" she asked. "Or did you tell them you were taking me to dinner?"

He glanced over to see she'd crossed her legs and the sight of her bare calf made him want to reach out and glide his hand over the smooth skin.

"I did tell them," he said. "Oliver was thrilled and Joshua seemed okay with it."

"The night you three came out to see Comet and Star, I felt like Joshua was warming up to me a bit. But I get the feeling he's not ready for his father to be…dating. Me— or any woman."

Win shrugged. "He's a teenager. He's moody. One minute he's happy and easygoing and the next he thinks the sky is falling in on him. But you shouldn't worry about Joshua not liking you. I'm fairly certain he does."

She smiled at him. "I can't ask for more than that."

"So what's been going on with your family since we visited the Bonnie B? Has your brother-in-law heard any news about Winona Cobbs?"

"Sadly, no." She shook her head with disbelief. "How does a ninety-seven-year-old woman just vanish without someone seeing her? And if she's been kidnapped, there's been no request for ransom. It's a real mystery. And each day that goes by, the more Stanley grieves and worries."

"Hmm. Could be she truly did get cold feet about walking down the aisle."

Frowning, she said, "I'll never believe that happened. Winona was crazy about Stanley. And I feel so sorry for him. He and Winona attended many of the special events in Bronco. If she wasn't missing, the two of them would be planning to go to the Gold Buckle Rodeo next month, and last year they were showing off Winona's engagement ring at the Bronco Harvest Festival. Now, without her, I doubt Stanley will want to attend either function."

"Well, let's keep our fingers crossed that she'll show up or someone will find her," Win replied. "I'd honestly like to meet the woman."

She laughed softly and Win realized he'd missed the warm sound as much as he'd missed hearing her voice and feeling the touch of her hand.

"You don't actually believe that psychic stuff, do you?" she asked.

"No. But I think some people have strong intuitions that happen to come true." He looked at her and grinned. "When I was a kid, there was a woman who lived alone in a cabin just beyond the north boundary of our ranch. Everyone called her a gypsy and, supposedly, she could read your palm or look at the cards and foretell your future. I didn't much go for any of that, but I sure thought she was beautiful. She had waist-length black hair and black eyes, and she wore layers of beads around her neck and wrists. I was in love."

"What happened to this woman?" she asked curiously. "Is she still there?"

"No. She moved away. No one seemed to know where she went or why she left. I guess you could say she was like Winona and just disappeared."

"Aww, that's kind of sad." She cast him an impish smile. "So when did you decide you liked women without the long black hair and layers of beads?"

"When I met a blond-haired teacher with tiny gold birds hanging from her earlobes," he said with a husky chuckle.

Frowning slightly, she touched a finger to her earlobe. "Was I wearing my little gold bird earrings when I met you?"

He nodded. "They dangled when you moved your head. Very pretty."

She reached over and clasped her hand around his. "It's nice of you to remember. To be honest, I never thought you noticed things like...well, my earrings."

With a wry laugh, he said, "In other words, I don't come across as a romantic type of guy." He glanced over to see a sheepish expression on her face.

"Not exactly," she answered. "But that's okay. I hardly come across as a glamour girl. We are who we are and that should be enough."

Squeezing her fingers, he said, "You look beautiful tonight. And I don't need or want a glamour girl."

A faint smile touched her lips as she looked at him. "I don't expect you to be the flower-and-poetry kind, either. As long as you want my company, that's enough."

He wanted more than her company. He wanted all of her. But he wasn't sure she was ready to take their relationship to an intimate level.

Shouldn't you be asking yourself if you're ready, Win? Are you ready to share more than talk and kisses with Stacy?

The questions waltzing through the back of his mind were annoying, but tonight Win was determined to push them aside. He was so weary of weighing every step he took. He was tired of trying to decide what was good or bad for him and his sons. For tonight, he simply wanted to be a man enjoying a warm and beautiful woman.

When they reached the outskirts of town, Win pulled into a parking lot and stopped the truck beneath the glow of a streetlamp. With the slim hope they could still make a reservation somewhere, he called several local restaurants, but after a few minutes, he put down the phone and slanted her a dismal look.

"No vacant tables. No cancellations," he said ruefully. "I'm really sorry, Stacy. It's too late for us to have a fancy dinner where we could have wine and a little secluded table with a linen tablecloth. Man, I've really turned this date into a fiasco. This will be one you won't forget."

She reached over and curled her fingers gently around

his forearm. "You're right. I won't forget it. And not because we're going to settle for something less than fancy. But because this is our first date and I'm with you. That's enough for me. So please quit beating yourself up over this."

With a helpless twist to his lips, he leaned across the console and pressed a kiss to her cheek. "I'll make this up to you. I promise."

"You just did, Win."

His green eyes were soft as they slowly scanned her face, and she held her breath, certain he was going to give her a full-fledged kiss on the lips, but after a moment, he cleared his throat and straightened back in his seat.

"We'd better go find something to eat. You're starving and so am I."

For the next twenty minutes, Win drove through town, passing all the restaurants they were both familiar with, but most of them appeared to be filled to the brim with evening diners.

Finally, Stacy said, "Look, Win, why don't we just do fast food? I'm almost to the point of settling for raw macaroni!"

He shot her an amused look. "That might be a little too crunchy for my taste. And think about it, Stacy. We deal with kids all day long. Any fast-food joint tonight will be running over with kids. I doubt we could hear ourselves think much less be able to talk to each other in a normal tone."

"You're right," she said glumly and then suddenly snapped her fingers as a thought struck her. "I know where we can eat, Win. The Gemstone Diner. Are you familiar with the place?"

His expression brightened as he nodded. "On Commercial Street down in Bronco Valley? That's a great idea! We should have thought about the diner earlier. It's not fancy, but the food is good." He grinned. "And I'm pretty sure the macaroni there will be cooked."

Stacy chuckled. "I can't wait."

Minutes later, when they entered the diner, they found the place busy but not so packed they couldn't find a booth at the back of the room. As they walked through the crowd of diners, Stacy noticed several people glancing at them. No doubt they were wondering what she was doing wearing velvet and pearls to a diner. Especially with her date wearing jeans and a denim jacket.

"It's not a linen tablecloth," he joked, "but it's clean."

The vinyl bench-type seats were big enough to seat four with two on each side of the table. When Stacy slid onto one of the benches, she expected Win to take a seat across from her. Instead, he chose to sit beside her, and the closeness of his body next to hers was enough to make her heart flutter.

Smiling at him, she murmured, "This is nice."

"What? The country music playing in the background? Or the rattling dishes behind the bar?"

She placed her hand over his. "Neither. I'm talking about us sitting close together."

His lips took on a wry slant as his gaze traveled over her face. "It's about time we had a chance to sit close together. Don't you think?"

"Definitely. And this booth is just as cozy as one of those ritzy tables you wanted."

"Only we don't have the wine," he pointed out.

"We'll get that later."

He arched a questioning look at her just as the waitress appeared with glasses of iced water and plastic-coated menus. After that, the mention of wine was forgotten as they studied the list of meals offered by the diner.

Both of them ended up ordering hamburgers, fries and milkshakes, and they shared a laugh when the platters of food and shakes were finally sitting in front of them.

"This is not a two-fork dinner," he said.

"No, this is good ol' finger food. And it's delicious. Especially when you're hungry."

Actually, Stacy could've been eating charred wood and she probably wouldn't have known it. And even if they had that bottle of wine he'd talked about, her spirits couldn't have soared any higher. No, she was happy because Win was sitting so close to her that their thighs were pressed together and the sides of their arms brushed with each bite they lifted to their mouths. And he was smiling at her. A real smile that said he was just as happy to be with her.

Ever since Win had called and invited her to dinner, Stacy had tried not to put too much meaning into his motivation. Taking her on a date didn't mean he'd had a sudden change of heart about the two of them having a deeper relationship. But now, as they sat close together and chatted about anything and everything, she couldn't help but hope he was finally seeing them as a real couple.

"There was a diner back in Whitehorn that had great food. Until the management changed. After that, it was terrible," he said as he dipped a fry into a mound of ketchup. "But I didn't eat out all that much when I lived there. Mom and Dad were always inviting me and the boys over to eat with them. Just like your siblings drop in at the Bonnie B to eat dinner."

She took a sip of her soda. "Hmm. I imagine they miss you and their grandsons. Did they try to talk you out of moving to Bronco? I think if I decided to move away, my parents would do plenty of talking. Not that they try to tell us kids how to live our lives. It's just that they're accustomed to me being nearby and often staying over in the ranch house with them."

"The ranch house on the Bonnie B is a huge nest. I get the idea your parents aren't the sort to hover over you. As for my parents, they kept advising me to think long and hard before I sold my ranch in Whitehorn and quit my teaching job there. But I finally managed to convince them it was the right thing for me to do." His gaze met hers as he reached for his soft drink. "Do you remember when I drove you home that night your car was on the blink? And during Oliver's chatter about our move from Whitehorn, he brought up a woman named Tara?"

Trying not to appear surprised, she nodded. "I do. I didn't ask who she was because…well, it wasn't any of my business."

He grimaced. "I told you then that I moved because I needed a change, and that much was true enough. But Oliver was right. We also left Whitehorn because of Tara. She was my girlfriend—for a while."

"I suspected something like that," Stacy admitted. "What happened? She ended things and broke your heart?"

"Hell no! Nothing like that," he said then quickly apologized. "Sorry, Stacy. I didn't mean to curse. It's just that… well, I was never emotionally close enough to Tara to get my heart broken. But she sure damaged my life."

"If you weren't in love with her, then how did she damage your life?"

His expression grim, he said, "It's a long story. You see, when I first started dating her, she was fun to be around and not fussy or demanding. Which made her a fit for me because all I wanted was someone to spend time with."

"Was she the first girl you dated after your wife passed away?"

"Yes. It took years for me to finally decide I needed to socialize and try to date again. But when I asked Tara out, dating was all I had in mind. I wasn't ready for anything serious with the woman. But she and everyone else in Whitehorn, it seems, had the idea that widowers are always itching to get married again. I think she believed that if we continued to date, I would eventually ask her to marry me."

"But you didn't."

"No way. I had no intention of marrying her. She was fun as dates go, but even if I'd wanted a wife, she wasn't what I considered wife material."

Frowning, Stacy took another sip of her soda. "I don't understand, Win. You broke up with her. I can't see why that forced you to leave Whitehorn. Was the experience with Tara that bad?"

He released a heavy breath. "You're probably thinking I'm some sort of helpless wimp. But you see, Tara was hard to ignore. She worked as the receptionist in the principal's office at the high school where I taught agribusiness. We had many mutual friends and acquaintances, so the word *bad* doesn't begin to describe the hell she put me through."

She looked at him in wonder as the French fry she was about to pop into her mouth paused in midair. "You make the ordeal sound terrible."

He twisted around on the seat to face her. "I need to start at the beginning so you'll understand. Tara and I dated about three months and, during that time, I suppose she started thinking that was more than enough time for me to pop the question. By the time Thanksgiving arrived, she and her parents were expecting me to show up with an engagement ring. When that didn't happen, Tara was furious. She threw a walleyed fit."

"And showed her true colors," Stacy replied while trying to imagine Win dealing with such a woman.

"I'd never seen that side of Tara and I didn't hesitate to tell her I wanted her out of my life. Things should've ended right then and there, but she refused to forgive and forget. She was out for blood. Her main goal in life turned into ruining mine."

Frowning, Stacy asked, "What did she do? Begin stalking you?"

"No. She was more insidious than that. She started telling our friends and colleagues at school that I had been stringing her along, playing her for a fool for my own entertainment. According to her, I had purposely and ruthlessly broken her heart. To put it simply, she painted me as a no-good jerk who had no business teaching a group of impressionable teenagers."

She stared at him in disbelief. "Win, I can't imagine any woman being so vindictive. More than that, I can't imagine your friends and coworkers believed such garbage."

Grimacing, he said, "You'd have to know Tara to understand. She had a charming way of making people like and trust her. Anyway, after weeks of her spreading lies, only a few of my closest friends took my side of things. The rest turned their back on me. People I'd worked with for years looked at me like I was a creep. Eventually, it became unbearable to go to work and try to avoid being shunned as though I had a contagious disease."

"Oh my. You must have felt so hurt and betrayed."

"It was very hurtful losing friends that I believed were loyal to me. It also made me angry. But eventually, after I took the time to think the matter through, I decided I'd not really lost anything because they obviously weren't true friends in the first place."

She nodded. "I'd see it the same way. A true friend doesn't desert you. They stand by you no matter what."

He shrugged his muscular shoulder. "Sometimes I wonder, Stacy, if I mishandled the whole incident. For sure, I should've never gotten involved with Tara. But to my friends and coworkers, I should've stood up and defended myself. Instead, I kept quiet, thinking it would all blow over."

As her gaze slipped over his rugged features, she could only imagine the hurt and frustration he must have gone through. "And when it didn't blow over, you decided moving away was the best thing to do."

He nodded. "I suppose plenty of folks would call that the coward's way out. But, ultimately, I was thinking of my sons. My hide was tough enough to deal with a slashed reputation, but my boys are still very young and impressionable. I want them to be proud of their father and be able to respect the man I am."

Smiling, she reached to fold her fingers around his hand. "You want to know what I think?"

His gaze locked with hers and, at that moment, Stacy was hardly aware of the people sitting nearby or the sounds of conversation and laughter in the background. Her entire focus was on him and what he could possibly be thinking. Not only about his escape from Whitehorn, but what this night might come to mean to the two of them.

"I do want to hear your thoughts," he murmured.

She breathed deeply. There were so many things about his life back in Whitehorn she'd like to hear about. And so many questions she'd like to ask him about his late wife. But now wasn't the right time, she thought. The last thing she wanted to do was come across to him as intrusive or pushy. "Okay. On one hand, I hate that you went through such a horrible ordeal. But, on the other, I'm really glad that you decided you had to move away from Whitehorn. And you chose Bronco for your new home. Otherwise, we would've never met. And that's too sad to think about."

She could see a smile in his eyes long before it ever reached his lips, and the sight was like sunshine peeking through a storm cloud.

Lowering his lips close to her ear, he said, "Okay. Once we finish eating, what would you like to do? I hope you're going to say you want to go somewhere nice and quiet and private."

Her pulse was suddenly thudding with eager anticipation. "I couldn't agree more. And I know just the place," she told him. "My parents have a guest cabin on the ranch. Nothing fancy. Just a little two-room log house with a great view of the mountains."

"No one is using it now?" he asked.

She shook her head. "About the only time it's ever used is when Mom wants to get Dad away from ranch work for one night."

"Sounds perfect," he said with a sly grin. "We'll pick up a bottle of wine on our way."

And once they were at the cabin would she end up in his arms? The mere thought made her inwardly shiver with anticipation.

Chapter Ten

Thirty minutes later, Win steered the truck over one of the several graveled roads on the Bonnie B, while Stacy navigated him to the cabin.

"I didn't realize this little guest lodge was going to be so close to the big house," he said as he noticed the lights of the ranch house glittering through a grove of evergreen trees.

"Well, the cabin is a guest house and you don't want to put your guests way out in the boonies," she teased. "But don't worry. My parents won't know we're at the cabin. And even if they did, they wouldn't care. I am a grown woman, after all."

He glanced over at her while his stomach made a funny little flip. "Yes, I have noticed," he said in a husky voice. "I've more than noticed."

She leveled a pointed look at him. "I wonder. If I hadn't kissed you that day in the park, I might still be waiting for you to take notice."

He chuckled. "You kissed me? I thought it was the other way around."

She laughed along with him and instead of feeling the bumps in the road, Win felt sure they were floating on air.

"Well, maybe it was a mutual thing," she said then pointed to a dim road leading off to their right. "Turn here. The cabin is at the end of this short lane."

Two minutes later, he stopped the truck near a small log structure with a tin roof and a tiny porch that sheltered the front door. Stepping stones led up to the porch, while a giant blue spruce stood on the east side of the house and a grove of a mixture of evergreens shrouded the west side. As they made their way to the house, a cool brisk wind blew through the tree branches and filled the air with the pungent scent of juniper.

Shivering slightly, she snuggled closer to his side and Win tightened his arm around her waist to keep her anchored there.

"It's a bit chilly tonight," she said. "We'll have to build a fire."

He very nearly groaned out loud. She'd built a fire in him from the moment her lips had first touched his and since then he'd tried, but miserably failed, to cool his thoughts of making love to her.

"I see a chimney so there must be a fireplace," he commented. "Is there firewood stored around the place?"

"Always," she answered. "Dad makes sure the hands never let the woodbox get empty."

As soon as they stepped into the cabin, Stacy flipped on a lamp then closed the heavy, wood-plank door behind them. Win glanced around the room that was furnished with two armchairs and a long couch. All of which were covered in nubby rust-colored fabric.

Spotting a low wooden table jammed between the chairs, he walked over and set down the bottle of wine he'd purchased before they'd left town.

"Mom comes up here fairly often and keeps the place dusted and swept." Stacy bent at the waist to open the screen on a small fireplace built into the east wall of the room. Once she straightened, she gestured to a woodbox sitting in a far corner.

He grabbed an armload of wood and brought it over. "Why don't you let me take care of it? I'm an old hand at building fires," he told her.

"Thanks for the offer, but I can start the fire. It's all ready with paper and kindling. All I need to do is tee-pee the logs and stick a match to it. I'll do that while you open the wine." She pointed to a short row of cabinets in the back corner of the room. "If you need an opener, there should be one over there in that drawer, and glasses are in the cabinet."

While she dealt with the fireplace, Win hung his jacket on a peg on the wall then opened the bottle of chilled wine. After searching through one of the cabinets, he found two squatty goblets and poured a generous amount in each one.

"Someone must enjoy wine when they visit this cabin," he said. "I found a pair of goblets."

"My parents. They think of this place as a romantic get-away without the travel expense," she said with a chuckle.

"I'd say you have smart parents."

"You've probably already noticed how much they adore each other. In some ways, they've treated each day of their married life as a honeymoon. That kind of devotion doesn't come along every day." She turned away from the fireplace and glanced in his direction. "It doesn't take long for the fire to warm up this small room. Unless it's subzero or blizzard weather. But the cabin is rarely used in such bad weather."

Marriage. Devotion. Win was glad she'd moved on from those subjects. Or was he? Maybe he needed to know if she was considering their relationship in those terms.

And what would you do if she was? Tell her you never

want to see her again? Face it, Win. You've reached the point of no return.

Shoving the heckling voice out of his head, he carried both glasses over to where she stood.

When he offered her one of them, she said, "Let me get out of this coat first."

He waited for her to slip off the garment and, while she placed it on the back of one of the chairs, he used the moment to take in her slender silhouette. Unlike his late wife and Tara, who'd both had tall, sturdy builds, Stacy was petite, her curves delicate. And he found everything about her figure incredibly alluring.

"There. That's better," she said.

She reached for one of the glasses and he handed it over.

"Should we make a toast?" he asked impishly.

She flashed him a coy smile. "We should definitely make a toast. To this special night."

He touched his glass to hers. "It started out on rough footing, but it's ending nicely."

She said, "I'll drink to that."

She tilted the glass to her lips and as Win watched her sip the dark liquid, he realized he didn't really want the wine. All he wanted was her.

Lowering her glass, she asked, "Why aren't you drinking with me?"

"Uh... I— I'm too busy looking at you."

She laughed softly and he could see she was taking his compliment lightly. That was hardly a surprise. Since he'd gotten to know her, he'd learned that she didn't think of herself as beautiful or sexy. And that was a shame because she was both those things and more. Much more.

"You kept insisting you wanted us to have wine on this date," she said. "Now you're totally disinterested."

He purposely tilted the glass to his lips and, after taking a short drink, set the glass on the table between the chairs. As he walked over to a window looking out the front of the cabin, she followed and something inside him quivered as her soft, flowery scent drifted up to him.

"It's quiet here," he remarked. "All I hear is the wind in the trees."

"The solitude is one of the things I love about the place. Sometimes, after I've had a really hectic day at school with the kids shrieking and shouting more than usual, I come up here and soak up the quietness. It recharges me."

A crescent moon had risen since they'd entered the cabin and the silvery light illuminated the stretch of ground leading to a patch of thick woods. It was an eerie but beautiful sight and Win thought how it somehow matched the unfamiliar feelings swirling inside him.

"I know what you mean. Teenagers can be mean and sarcastic even when they don't know they're being mean and sarcastic. It gets hard to deal with at times. But then I think about how they need to learn and how an education will help to build their lives, and I'm able to push the stress of teaching aside." He looked thoughtfully down at her as an image of his student Julie flashed in his mind. "Is there ever a child, or multiple children in your class, you worry about?"

"You mean about their ability to learn? Or worry about their home life?"

"Home life."

Her sigh was a sound of regret. "Oh yes. There have been times I've discussed a child's physical condition with the school nurse and, once, I reported a disturbing incident to the principal about a child being left home alone. I don't know how you feel about such things, but I want to step in and make a fuss—to make sure every child is loved and cared for. But in the end, Win, we can't always do that because they're not our children. So we merely have to do the best we can."

Her words touched him far more than she could ever guess and, without thinking, he curved his arm around her shoulders and turned her so that she was facing him.

"You just said everything I feel, Stacy. And I… I don't know how to say it, except that I think we're kindred spirits."

Her palms came up to rest against his chest while her lashes lowered to hide most of her blue eyes. "It's hard for me to believe you think that, Win. I mean yes, we're both teachers and we both choose to work in the classroom for the same reasons. But I'm not a typical ranch girl."

"What's that got to do with anything?"

"Ranching is your life," she said quietly. "I heard Joshua talking about how well his mother could ride a horse and I imagine Yvette was capable of doing other things around the ranch."

"I don't want a ranch hand, Stacy. I want a woman," he told her.

Her lips twisted to a rueful slant as she glanced at him. "When we were first getting to know each other, you told me you didn't want a woman. Period."

His hands wrapped both her shoulders and the warmth of her flesh seeping into his fingers made him want to move them over the rest of her body, to have her curves filling his palms.

"That's what I thought," he said huskily. "But you're beginning to change my mind."

She released a shaky breath and Win slid his right hand downward until he reached the spot just above her left breast. He could feel her heart thumping at a rapid pace, but it wasn't racing nearly as fast as his.

"I don't know what to say to that," she said in a voice just above a whisper. "Or what to think."

Positioning his hands at the small of her back, he pulled her against him and her head lolled back as she looked up at him. He could see questions marching across her face and in her eyes. Questions that he wasn't ready to answer. Not to her or himself.

"I don't know what to think about it, either," he said. "But I can tell you what I'm feeling right now. I want you very much. If that isn't enough, I—"

His words paused as her forefinger reached up to touch the middle of his bottom lip.

"It's more than enough, Win." Rising on the tips of her toes, she tilted her face to his. "Can't you see how much I want you? Can't you feel it when you touch me?"

Groaning, he lowered his mouth close to hers. "When I touch you, I feel fire and pleasure, and all kinds of things that are too good to describe."

"Mmm. All I feel is desire," she confessed. "The desire to be closer to you, to give all of myself to you. It's like nothing I've ever felt before."

"Stacy. Stacy."

Breathing her name was all he could manage before he closed the tiny space between their lips, and once he began to kiss her, he realized no more words were necessary. There were plenty of other ways he could convey the desire coursing through his body.

His lips searched hers until the connection turned to hungry need and his tongue was delving into her mouth, his teeth nipping at her lips. She responded with a fervor that shocked him and sent his desire skyrocketing to an even higher level.

If it hadn't been for the need of oxygen, he would've kept on kissing her, but his burning lungs demanded that he lift his head. When he finally eased back from her, he saw that her eyes were closed and her lips were swollen. The pink lipstick she'd been wearing was now only a memory, but there was plenty of rosy color glowing on her cheeks and Win could only think he'd never seen a more beautiful woman in his life.

Her eyes fluttered open at the same time her fingers reached out to gently touch his cheek. "Win, I think it's time I showed you the bedroom."

A ball of emotion suddenly formed in the middle of his chest and spread upward to his throat. "Stacy, are you sure about this? Me?"

His voice sounded like he'd been eating gravel and his hands trembled as they moved against her back. Something was happening to him, he thought. Something strange and wild and wonderful.

"I realize if you count the days we've known each other, it wouldn't be all that many. And some people might say we've not been together nearly long enough to make love. But I feel like I've known you forever. I feel like I've been waiting for years for you to come into my life. Now that you have, I don't want to wait any longer."

As his gaze roamed her lovely face, he told himself he wasn't going to think about what she might be expecting from him. Or even what he expected from himself. The only thought he was going to allow into his brain was this moment, this night, and her.

"Neither do I."

His words barely made it past his tight throat, but she

managed to hear them and she responded by folding her hand around his and leading him away from the window.

They passed through a door located behind the kitchen area and into a bedroom just big enough to hold a double bed and one chest of drawers. Two windows were on the east wall, allowing fingers of moonlight to slant across the quilt covering the bed.

"I hope you weren't expecting a fancy suite," she said with a husky laugh. "Because this is only basic comfort."

Laughing with her, he snaked an arm around her waist and pulled her tight against him. "Funny girl. As if I have comfort on my mind." Raising a hand, he smoothed his fingers over the wave of blond hair at her temple. "You know, before we met, I had practically forgotten how to laugh."

Her hands slid up to the ridges of his shoulders. "I must be having a positive effect on you."

"Hmm. You're having all kinds of effects on me, my beautiful lady." As soon as he whispered the last word, he covered her lips with his and the sweet contact sent a flash of fire straight to his brain.

Stacy reacted by quickly deepening the kiss and, in a matter of seconds, Win's senses were flying around the room, making it impossible to think about anything but getting her undressed and into his arms.

When their lips finally parted, she looked up at him with smoky-blue eyes that struck something deep within him.

"You can't know how much I want you, Win," she whispered. "It's scandalous, and I should be embarrassed to admit it to you. But my desire for you isn't something I want to hide. I want to show it to you. Over and over."

She was saying things to him he'd never expected to hear. Touching him in ways that shattered the barrier he'd long erected around his heart. Each time their lips met, every time she touched him, he felt a part of himself breaking. The feeling was both thrilling and frightening. It was also something he couldn't stop. Even if he wanted to.

"My Stacy. My sweet, sweet Stacy."

He placed another long kiss on her lips before urging her over to the side of the bed. When he reached for the tied sash on the side of her waist, she smiled and pushed his hands aside.

"This dress is complicated to get in and out of," she explained. "It might be better if I do mine and you do yours. Okay?"

He chuckled under his breath as he began to shed his shirt and jeans. "You think I'm going to complain about that? As long as we're lying together on that bed in the next two minutes, I'll be a happy man."

"Two minutes, huh? I'll bet I'll be there before you are."

As soon as her dare was out, clothes, boots and high heels began flying. Eventually, Stacy hit the mattress a few seconds before Win and, as he stretched out beside her, she made a triumphant fist pump.

"I'm the winner," she announced.

Rolling onto his side, he reached out and touched a hand to one small perky breast. The pink nipple instantly hardened against his callused palm.

"You look even more beautiful without your clothes," he murmured. "Beautiful and perfect."

"So do you."

He closed his eyes as she trailed her fingers along his arm then onto his chest and down to his navel. Rivulets of fire followed in the wake of her touch and he wondered how he was supposed to survive the heat and the sheer need that was quickly beginning to consume him.

"No. Nothing about me is perfect, Stacy. But if you want me, the rest doesn't matter."

Her hands cupped his jaw then slid upward until her fingers were thrust into his hair. "Everyone has flaws. That's why we need each other. That's why we can be so good for each other."

"Good, yes." He leaned his head forward and, with his eyes still closed, placed a kiss on her forehead, the tip of her nose and the bottom of her chin. "So very, very good."

She sighed and her soft breath fanned the side of his face. The sensation was just as erotic as the touch of her hand and, with a needy groan, he buried a hand in the hair at the back of her head and drew her mouth to his.

The kiss went on and on until her slender body arched into his and her fingers began to dig into the flesh on his back. When he finally pulled his head from hers, they were both panting for air.

Sliding one leg over his hips, she said, "If you kiss me like that again, I'm going to break apart."

The glow he saw on her face was more radiant than the flames in the fireplace and he was mesmerized by the sparkle in her eyes, the pink color on her cheeks and lips. How had he not noticed before that she was so stunning, so utterly desirable? Had he deliberately been keeping his eyes shut because he'd been afraid of her? Of this?

No. He wasn't going to question himself now. He wasn't going to think. He was only going to feel.

"You won't break apart because you're going to be right here in my arms and I'll hold you together."

His hand slipped between the juncture of her thighs and when he touched the moist folds of her womanhood, he thought he might be wrong. He might be the one breaking into helpless pieces.

"Oh, Win. Win. Make love to me."

"It'll be my pleasure. My deepest pleasure," he whispered against her lips. Then suddenly his head came up and he stared at her in astonishment. "I think— Oh, Stacy. I wasn't thinking about you and me like this. I don't have a condom with me and I doubt your father has any extra laying around the cabin."

She chuckled. "If he does, my mother might think it a little suspicious. Anyway, there's no need for you to worry about a condom. I'm on oral contraceptives."

He arched a brow at her. "For real?"

The naughty grin she gave him was another surprise.

"Yes. But not for the obvious reason. I take them for other reasons—medical purposes—but I'm protected just the same."

Groaning with relief, he eased his head down next to hers. "Guess it's easy for you to figure out why I don't carry a condom in my wallet. I don't have a need for one," he said wryly.

"I don't think either one of us needs to apologize or feel embarrassed for not having an active sex life. Do you?"

With a hand in her hair, he tugged her close enough to place a kiss on her forehead. "Like I said, we're kindred spirits."

Her arm slipped around his neck. "And we're together."

Together. For how long? How long would he be allowed to feel this much pleasure?

The dark, uninvited thoughts caused him to pause. But a split second was all the time it took to push them aside and pull her into the tight circle of his arms.

"Yes. Together."

He whispered the words against her lips before he turned the contact into a fiery kiss that blocked everything from his mind, except her.

* * *

His mouth sliding over her skin, his hands touching the secret parts of her body was like a match setting fire to every cell in her body. All Stacy could think about was having him inside her, moving with her in that age-old dance of love.

When he finally rolled her onto her back and parted her thighs, she was desperate to have her body connected to his. And as soon as his hard shaft entered her, she arched her hips upward to take him deeper toward the ache that only he could ease.

The movement caused him to groan and she opened her eyes to see his jaw clamped as though he was in fierce pain.

Touching fingertips to his face, she gently whispered, "Win, is something wrong?"

His expression was a mixture of pleasure and pain as he looked down at her. "Oh, Stacy, I— Nothing is wrong. It's just that I want you so much it hurts."

"Let me take the hurt away."

Placing her hand at the back of his neck, she pulled his head down to hers and touched her lips to his. As she kissed him, she heard a needy growl deep in his throat and then his hips began moving in slow, steady thrusts that filled her with wave after wave of pleasure.

After that, everything became a blur as they strained to keep their lips together and their hands free to roam the other's heated flesh. Over and over, he plunged into her, his pace quickening with each passing moment, and she did her best to keep up with him.

But after a while, the need in her became so great she thought she would burst. As if he understood, he reached beneath her hips and pulled them tightly against his, and an explosion erupted inside her. Lights flashed behind her eyes and suddenly her whole body felt as if it were floating off the bed.

Crying out his name, she clutched his arms and then she heard him grunt with relief as he spilled himself inside her.

Stacy was still dragging in deep, ragged breaths when her senses finally gathered enough for her to become aware of her surroundings. And even then, she wasn't convinced the walls of the little bedroom had quit spinning. But the weight of Win's warm body draped over hers felt very real and very wonderful, and just so he wouldn't move away too soon, she wrapped her arms around him.

Against her breast, she could feel the heavy thud of his heart and the rise and fall of his chest as he struggled to regain his breath. And in that moment, she knew without a doubt, that she loved him. He was the man she wanted to spend the rest of her life with. He was the only man she would ever invite into her heart. The certainty of her feelings filled her with a peace and joy she'd never felt before.

She turned her head and nuzzled her cheek to the side of his face. How nice it would be, she thought, to wake up in the morning and feel the shadow of his beard against her cheek.

"I hope you feel as good as I do right now," she murmured.

Shifting his weight off her, he propped his head on his hand and slowly studied her face. "Good? Stacy, you can't know…" Pausing, he drew in a deep breath before he continued. "You can't know what I'm feeling right now. I'm not even sure I know myself."

He didn't sound exactly euphoric or as blissful as she was feeling. But maybe sex was mundane for him, she thought. After all, he'd been married for eight years. Or maybe he'd just not felt the same incredible connection she'd felt to him while they'd been making love.

Making love. Yes. In her mind, she'd been making love to Win for weeks now. But did he view what they'd just shared as love? She wanted to think so. But not for anything would she try to pull that word from him; it had to come from his own free will. Because it was his true feelings and not just a way to appease her.

She gave him a tender smile. "Don't worry about it. I'm feeling enough for both of us."

His expression somber, he lifted a fingertip to her cheek and traced lazy circles upon her damp skin.

"Yes, I think you are. And—" With a helpless grunt, he pressed his lips to her temple. "You're incredible, Stacy. You truly are. But I—think we should get dressed and be leaving."

Leaving! What was he thinking? That being this close to her wasn't right for him? That *she* wasn't right for him? The idea tore at her heart. "Get dressed and leave?" she asked hoarsely. "Why?"

Even as she asked the question, he was easing out of her arms and swinging his legs over the side of the bed. "I just—think it's best. For the both of us."

Maybe he thought it best to end their night together, but to her it was devastating. Could she have been so wrong in thinking he'd kissed her, made love to her with deep, genuine feelings? To think she might have misjudged him so badly caused a shaft of fear to shoot through her. She'd made mistakes in the past, but this time with Win, she'd instinctively trusted her heart to him. Had she made another terrible mistake?

"I don't understand. I thought—" Pausing, she shook

her head. "What we had a few moments ago was special. You didn't think so?"

He cleared his throat and, without looking her way, reached for his clothing on the floor. "I told you a moment ago, Stacy, that I—don't understand what I'm thinking or feeling."

Obviously he was trying to tell her that any feelings he had for her weren't cut and dried. If there were any feelings at all, she thought grimly.

"So this has all been too fast for you?" she asked, unable to keep sarcasm from edging into her voice. "I wonder why you weren't concerned about the speed of things before we went to bed together?"

He slanted her an awkward glance. "I should've been. I wasn't thinking. I, uh, really wasn't planning on this—or staying all night. I imagine you knew that."

If he'd pulled a knife and stabbed her directly in the heart, she doubted she would've been more hurt or shocked than she was now. "No," she said in an incredulous voice. "I didn't know. Didn't you say the boys were staying over at your friend's place tonight?"

"Yes. But I need to, uh, check on some things at the ranch."

He stood and stepped into his jeans and Stacy had to fight the urge to yell at him.

"Lucky for you that you happened to suddenly remember these…things you need to do," she said, unable to keep a touch of bitterness from her voice.

"I'm sorry, Stacy. I hadn't planned on this happening."

Apparently not, she thought sickly. He'd had sex with her and now, for some reason she couldn't begin to fathom, he regretted it.

Drawing on all the patience she possessed, she said,

"Sounds like you didn't plan on staying or leaving. Just what were you planning for this evening, Win?"

He zipped the fly on his jeans then stooped to pick up his shirt. "I don't know. I just have to go. Can't you leave it at that?"

He might as well have sloshed a bucket of ice water over her and, with her mouth set in a grim line, she climbed off the bed and began to dress.

So much for thinking she'd had a night full of bliss ahead of her. So much for getting the idea that Win actually felt something deep and real for her, she thought sickly.

Out in the living room, he hurriedly pulled on his jacket and hat while Stacy walked barefoot over to the fireplace and stood with her back to the flames.

"What are you doing?" he asked. "You can't go out without your shoes or coat."

"Not at this time of year," she replied then gestured to the bottle of wine he'd left sitting on the table. "Don't forget your wine. You might give it to Anthony as added payment for watching the boys for you."

He grunted. "Anthony only drinks beer. I'll leave the wine here. Maybe your parents will enjoy it."

"Okay." Her chest aching, she turned toward the fire to spare herself the sight of his miserable expression. "Drive safely going home. And thank you for dinner."

"I'm going to drive you home, Stacy. So get your coat and shoes."

She whirled around to stare at him. "Who do you think you are, Win Jackson? Just because you took me to bed doesn't mean you have the right to order me around. I have no intention of letting you drive me home. So leave. Go on and get back to the J Barb so you can get all those *things* done."

He walked over to where she stood. "I understand you're

angry with me, Stacy. You're thinking I'm acting like a
jerk. But I can't stay. Not now. And I'm not going to leave
you here. Alone."

A curt laugh erupted from her. "I've stayed in this cabin
alone many times. When I get ready to go home, I'll walk.
The ranch house is no more than a hundred yards right
through that stand of trees and there's a clear walking path
the whole way. I don't need a ride."

He stared at her for a few seconds longer and Stacy didn't
miss the anguish twisting his features, or the pain shadow-
ing his eyes. It was hurting him to leave, she realized. So
what was pushing him toward the door? If she only knew.

"Alright. Then I'll say good-bye."

"Good-bye, Win."

He left the cabin and moments later, Stacy heard the engine of his truck fire to life, but she didn't bother to glance
out the window to see if he was leaving. He'd already left
her before he'd ever climbed off the bed.

Chapter Eleven

"Dad, do you think Joshua will ever make the basketball team?"

Win looked over at Oliver, who was sitting next to him on the gymnasium bleachers as they watched the after-school basketball practice.

"All the boys are on the team," Win explained. "Are you asking if Joshua will make the *main* team?"

Oliver nodded. "Yeah. That's what I mean. Some of the junior and senior boys are really tall. I don't think Joshua can take their place."

"You have to have more than height to be good at basketball. Joshua understands it takes time and lots of hard work to earn a spot on a team," Win told him. "Your brother might not ever be a starter."

Oliver grimaced. "Then why bother with all this practicing? We could be home riding horses instead," he grumbled.

"Being a main player isn't the important thing here, Oliver," Win said patiently. "Joshua wants to be a part of something with his friends. Someday, when you get older, you'll understand."

Oliver's head tilted from one shoulder to the other as he considered his father's remarks. "Why do I always need to be older? I'm smart right now."

Any other time, Oliver's response would've drawn a chuckle from Win, but at the moment he didn't have the energy or the inclination to laugh. Not when everything inside him felt half dead.

He glanced at Oliver then out to the court where Joshua was passing the ball to a teammate. Without his sons, his life wouldn't have any meaning. They were the only things that kept him moving forward these days.

"Yes, you're smart," he said to Oliver. "But in five more years, you're going to be a whole lot smarter."

"Gosh, Dad, by then I might be a genius."

Forcing his lips to form a smile, he patted his son's shoulder. "I hope you are, Oliver. Then you can teach me."

He needed someone to teach him a thing or two, Win thought dully, because these days he seemed to be doing everything wrong. Ever since he'd left Stacy in the guest cabin, he'd felt worse than a jerk. He felt like half a man. A man too timid to step out of the shadows and into the sunshine.

The scoreboard buzzed to announce the end of the practice and, as the players put away their gear and headed to the locker room, Win and Oliver descended the bleachers and walked out to the lobby of the gymnasium to wait for Joshua.

After ten minutes passed without any sign of the teenager, Win was about to head back inside the gym to see what was keeping him, when Joshua suddenly walked into the lobby with Anthony at his side.

"Before you start barking, it's my fault that Joshua is late," Anthony told Win. "I made him wait until I could join him."

Win refrained from rolling his eyes. "Why? Is he in trouble?" he questioned.

Anthony chuckled then, seeing Win wasn't laughing, he gave him a pat on the shoulder. "Lighten up, buddy. Joshua is one of my best kids. And I'm not saying that because you and I are friends. I wanted to walk out with him so I could catch you before you left. I thought the four of us might go out and grab some burgers, my treat. What do you say?"

Win glanced toward a window near the entrance doors. "It's cold and rainy and we have chores waiting. I think—"

Anthony quickly interrupted. "I think that's all the more reason you need to eat before you go home to the ranch. That way you won't have to fix supper after you do your chores."

"Yeah, Dad! Let's eat with Anthony!" Oliver exclaimed. "He eats good stuff like burgers and pizza!"

"I'd like burgers tonight, too, Dad." Joshua added his opinion.

Win leveled a somber look at his sons. "If it was left up to Anthony, you'd be eating burgers or pizza every night."

"Oh, come on, Win. I'm not that bad," Anthony told him. "Besides, one night this week won't hurt."

"And it might make you smile, Dad." Oliver spoke up. "That won't hurt, either."

From the corner of his eye, he saw Anthony flash him a meaningful look, but he didn't glance his way. He was too stunned by Oliver's remark to worry about what Anthony was thinking. Had he been acting like a crank with his sons? He'd not thought so, but apparently Oliver had picked up on his father's unhappiness. The idea bothered him greatly. He didn't want his boys suffering just because their father had made a mess of things with Stacy.

"Okay," he conceded. "We'll go, but we can't stay in town for very long. Remember, the animals at the ranch are hungry, too."

"Yay! Burgers! Can I have a milkshake, too?" Oliver asked Anthony.

Anthony chuckled as the four of them passed through the double doors leading out of the building. "Why ask me? You'd better ask your dad," he told the boy.

"Well, I'm asking you because you're gonna be paying for everything," Oliver explained.

Anthony laughed again, but all Win could manage was a half-hearted grunt of amusement.

"As far as I'm concerned, you can have two milkshakes, Oliver. You're a growing boy," Anthony told him.

"Oliver, you always have to be a hog," Joshua goaded his brother.

"So what? Hogs are really smart," Oliver shot back at him. "And Dad just told me I was going to be a genius when I got older."

Joshua laughed at his little brother. "Now, you're fibbing, along with being a hog."

"I am not fibbing! Dad did say I might be a genius. Didn't you, Dad?"

"I did say you were going to get smarter. I think you put in the part about being a genius," Win answered.

Joshua snickered. "See. I knew you were fibbing."

"Oh yeah? Well, I'm the one who made straight A's on my report card! Not you!" Oliver boasted.

Win glanced over his shoulder at the bickering brothers. "It's raining. You two run on to the truck. And quit that darned arguing or we're going straight home."

As the boys trotted on to the truck parked at the far end of the parking lot, Anthony glanced over at him.

"They're just being typical brothers, Win."

"I know. It's just that I'm not in the mood to listen to it tonight. And if you think you're going to start lecturing me about Stacy, then you might as well forget it. I'm in no mood to listen to you, either."

Anthony merely chuckled at Win's sour warning. "This is going to be a fun meal for all."

"Who said anything about having fun? Is that what you think life is supposed to be? One big party?"

"All right. I've had enough," Anthony muttered.

He paused on the sidewalk and, before Win guessed what his friend was doing, he pulled out his cell phone.

"Joshua, this is Anthony. You and Oliver stay in the truck and wait. Your Dad and I will be there in a few minutes."

"What is this about?" Win asked.

With a hand on his shoulder, Anthony turned him in the direction of a red pickup parked several yards away from Win's.

"Since you don't want to talk over dinner, we'll talk right now in my truck," Anthony said flatly. "And I'm not in the *mood* to argue."

Win wanted to do more than argue. He wanted to walk away, but he knew the boys were most likely watching curiously out the window and he didn't want them to get the idea that something was amiss with their dad and his best friend.

Once both men were inside the dry confines of the truck cab, Win was the first to speak. "I've already told you, Anthony, I'm not going to have a discussion with you about Stacy."

"If you're not going to discuss the problem with me, then who are you going to discuss it with? Your brother?"

"No. I don't want him to know I've been a fool a second time."

Anthony gave him a hard look then nodded. "You know,

you're absolutely right about being a fool. You're probably the biggest one I've ever known."

"Thanks for being such a good buddy," Win said sarcastically. "I can always count on you to make me feel better."

"Damn it, I don't want you to feel better. I want you to face up to what you're doing."

Staring out the windshield, Win muttered, "And what do you think I'm doing? Slacking off on my job? Being a bad father?"

"You'd never do either of those things. But you sure don't have any qualms about running away from a woman."

"Listen, Anthony, I told you that Stacy and I went out to dinner."

"That's been nearly a week ago. And you've not seen her since."

Win stared at him. "How do you know? Have you been talking to her?"

Anthony cursed under his breath. "You think I'd talk about you behind your back? To a woman?"

Did he? No. Anthony might be assertive at times, but he respected Win's privacy.

"If you must know, Joshua mentioned it to me," Anthony explained. "I think your sons are wondering about you and her."

"Oh. I didn't know," Win mumbled then shrugged. "I need to tell them that…well, nothing serious is going to happen with me and Stacy. That way they won't be confused and wondering."

"Won't be confused? Pardon me, but even your children can see you're daffy about Stacy. You think they'll understand why you're suddenly running backward? I'm an adult and I don't understand. How do you expect the boys to comprehend your behavior?"

Win wiped a hand over his face at the same time he tried to wipe the image of Stacy's beautiful face out of his mind. He'd had to call upon every ounce of strength he possessed to leave the cabin with her face a picture of wounded misery. And he hated himself a thousand times over for hurting her. He'd never intended to cause her pain. He'd only wanted to love her. But then fear had taken him over and he'd run like a coward.

"Look, Anthony, having a woman in my life just won't work. I came to that conclusion the night Stacy and I went out to dinner. I have too many memories, too many worries and doubts that I can't shed. I'd only end up making her miserable and then losing her."

Memories. Yeah, this past week he'd been assaulted with memories of holding Stacy in his arms, kissing her giving lips and loving her. He'd been totally stunned by the feelings she'd evoked in him. Making love to her had transported him to a far off beautiful place. One that he'd never wanted to leave. But as soon as his senses had returned to reality and he'd glanced around the cozy bedroom of the cabin, fear had seized him. All he could think was that he had to get away from the happiness and pleasure Stacy was giving him. He couldn't let himself love and lose again.

The sound of Anthony letting out a long breath, pulled Win out of his bleak thoughts and he glanced over at his friend.

"You know, buddy, everyone has memories and worries that we have to deal with and push aside," Anthony told him. "I think it's the losing her that's getting to you. Yes, you're afraid of losing her. Not because you'd make her miserable. No, you're frightened of losing her the way you lost your wife."

"Damn right. Wouldn't you be?"

"Yes, I'm fairly sure I would be frightened. Because you couldn't stop or prevent Yvette's death. I understand all that. But if you keep hanging on to your fear, you might as well go sit in a dark corner and let Stacy find some other man who'd be thrilled to give her the love she needs."

The image of Stacy making love to another man made him sick inside and, without even knowing it, a rueful groan slipped out of him. "How am I supposed to get rid of this fear, Anthony?"

"I can't offer you a magic cure. I only know that you can't let it continue to define the man you are, or how you live the rest of your life." He reached over and affectionately punched his fist against Win's upper arm. "Come on. The boys are hungry and so am I. And, Win, you're going to get this right. I have faith in you."

With a hopeless grin, he looked over at Anthony. "Thanks for putting up with me."

"I expect you to do the same for me—if I ever make a fool of myself over a woman."

"Ha! I can't wait to see that," Win joked and, as the two men left the truck and walked over to join the boys, he realized this was the first time since he'd left Stacy at the cabin that he felt like he was, at least, half human.

Later that night, on the Bonnie B, Stacy was sitting at a small desk in her bedroom, going through a stack of artwork she'd assigned her students yesterday. She'd asked them to draw a picture of what the fall season meant to them and it was clear as she studied each paper that each child had their own special images. A pile of colorful leaves. A pumpkin. A cup of hot chocolate. A cat curled up on a rug. And then there was a red heart, so big that it nearly covered the whole sheet of paper. Obviously, the child was simply trying to say she loved everything about autumn.

She glanced at the girl's name at the bottom of the paper and even though Stacy wanted to smile, tears gathered in her eyes.

The evening Win had given her a ride home to the Bonnie B when her car had failed to start, she'd told him how fall was her favorite time of the year. As simple as that meeting between them had been that night, she'd felt a special connection to him. When she'd walked at his side, it had felt right and perfect. Had she been a fool then? Right from the very start?

"Knock, knock! Want some company?"

Robin's cheerful voice had her glancing around to see her sister's head peeping around the partially open door of her bedroom.

Hurriedly dashing away her tears with the back of her hand, Stacy stood and walked over to greet her. "I'm always happy to see my sister."

Robin kissed her cheek then stepped back to scrutinize her somber face.

"You taste salty."

Stacy avoided her sister's probing gaze. "It's the makeup I wore to school today. I've not cleaned my face yet."

"Is that what's making your eyes water, too?"

Grimacing, Stacy turned away from her, walked over to the bed and sat down on the side of the mattress. "I'm probably needing glasses. All the paperwork I go through puts a strain on my eyes."

"Strange that you're just now having a problem with eye strain." Robin walked over and sat next to her. "I think it's more of a heart strain problem."

Stacy stared at the floor as pain welled up in her chest.

For the past week, since she and Win had said goodbye, she'd tried to appear normal and go on with her daily life as though nothing had happened. But Win's sudden rejection had shattered her and, not surprisingly, her family and friends were beginning to notice her despondent mood.

"I'm okay, Robin. Just disappointed, that's all."

"In Win, you mean?"

She looked at her sister. "Yes. But even more disappointed in myself. I should've known right from the start that Win wasn't ready for a serious relationship with me or any woman. I must've had my head in the clouds to think he could put the loss of his wife behind him and begin a new life with me. Anyway, it's over between us." She made a mocking grunt. "My romance didn't last long, did it?"

Robin scowled at her. "How do you know it's over? Have you talked to Win?"

"No. He hasn't reached out to me and I'm certainly not going to call him. He's the one who walked out after we—" She broke off as images of her and Win making love flashed through her mind. Shaking away the memory, she started again. "He's the one who walked out during our date. He came up with a lame excuse about needing to do things on the ranch, but we both knew he simply wanted to leave."

Robin's scowl turned into a confused frown. "Why do you think he wanted to put an end to the evening? Did you two have a disagreement?"

Stacy released a heavy sigh. "I only wish it was something that simple. We could've talked through a simple disagreement. But this—it goes much deeper, Robin. At least, I think it does. There are times when I'm feeling sorry for myself that I think Win just doesn't care enough about me to want to keep our relationship going. But other times, when I'm trying to look at things clearly, I think the problem is tied to him losing his wife so unexpectedly and at such a young age. I'm just not sure he's ready to get seriously involved with anyone again. You see, he told me how, before he'd left Whitehorn, he'd finally decided to try dating again, but things turned very ugly with the woman when he wanted to keep things casual."

"I suppose she was expecting a proposal or something close to it?"

Stacy nodded. "Right. And he didn't want to get that involved with her. But now…well, I can only wonder if his past is still haunting him. Either that or he just isn't interested in me anymore."

"Hmm. Well, it's not unusual for a man to run scared if he thinks he's falling in love," Robin said.

Falling in love? Could her sister be right? This past week she'd relived over and over their night at the cabin and the moments she'd spent in Win's arms. She'd carefully studied all the words he'd spoken to her and, as perfect as their lovemaking had been, she'd not heard anything from him about being in love with her. Did she dare even think he might love her?

We're kindred spirits. When Win had spoken those words to her, she'd been lying in his arms and his lips had been pressed to her forehead. Even now, after this week of not hearing from him, she wanted to believe the emotion she'd heard in his voice. She longed to believe he'd kissed her and made love to her with his heart.

"Robin, do you honestly think he could be falling in love with me?" she asked then shook her head. "Sorry, I shouldn't have asked you such a question. You don't really know Win all that well. And you've not seen the two of us together. You couldn't know how he feels about me. I don't even know myself. But I want to think—" Her throat was suddenly aching with hot tears, forcing her to swallow before she could finish. "Foolish or not, I want to think there's a chance he could be falling in love with me."

Wrapping her arm around Stacy's shoulders, Robin gave her sister an encouraging squeeze.

"I think I gave you this advice before, but I'm going to give it to you again anyway. Give the man a bit more time, Stacy. He needs to come to terms with his past. And what he wants for his future."

Stacy gave her sister a lopsided grin. "In other words, call on my patience and wait."

Robin chuckled. "More or less. I happen to think Mr. Jackson is going to soon realize what a good thing he has in you."

"You're my sister. You're biased," Stacy said.

Robin rose and, grabbing both of Stacy's hands, pulled her to her feet. "I'm also dying for some of the hot chocolate Mom is making. Come on and have a cup with me. You need to get out of this room and put a smile on your face. Everything is going to work out, sissy. I'll make a wager that by the time Christmas arrives, you're going to be a very merry woman."

Doing her best to smile, Stacy planted a kiss on Robin's cheek. "Thank you, sweet sister. Now, let's go have that hot chocolate. I'm going to pile mine high with marshmallows and whipped cream."

Laughing, Robin ushered her toward the door. "Now you're talking."

The next afternoon, after classes had been dismissed for the day, Win walked out of the school building to start across the parking lot to his truck when he noticed Julie standing at the designated pickup spot on the sidewalk.

Since he'd noticed the girl boarding the bus before, he was surprised to see her waiting with a few of her classmates for their rides.

Pausing for a moment, he thought about walking over and quietly questioning her. Just to make sure her dad was in good enough condition to drive, but he didn't want to embarrass the girl, so he continued walking.

When someone tugged on his jacket from behind, he was more than surprised to see Julie had chased him down the sidewalk.

"I apologize for interrupting you, Mr. Jackson, but I thought you might be wondering why I wasn't riding the bus."

"I was wondering," he said. "Is everything okay, Julie? Is your father coming to pick you up?"

The smile that suddenly spread across her face was so out of character for the withdrawn student, he could only stare at her in wonder.

"Oh no. Dad isn't coming. He's at work. He got a different job. One he likes a lot more than the last one. My mom is picking me up. She's moved back home now and…well, everything is just so much better. And you know something, Mr. Jackson? The next time you have a field trip, I just might get to go!"

"That's great, Julie. I'm glad you told me."

A car honked and the girl glanced over her shoulder. "There she is now! See you tomorrow, Mr. Jackson!"

She took off in a run to where a dark-haired woman was waving a hand out the window, and Win stood there watching as the girl happily joined her mother.

Wonder of wonder, Win thought. There were still good things happening in world and to people who deserved better in their lives.

As he continued on to his truck, he realized how much he'd like to call Stacy and share Julie's good news. Not that she knew the girl or that Win had ever mentioned her troubled home life to Stacy. She wanted *all* children to be loved and cared for, no matter where they went to school or who taught them. Hearing that Julie's situation had improved would definitely put a smile on her face.

The image of Stacy's smiling face floated through his mind as he climbed into his truck and drove toward the elementary school to pick up Oliver.

Since Anthony had lectured him last night about Stacy, Win had been thinking about all his friend had said. Especially the part about Joshua and Oliver being confused about their father's behavior.

At school, Win had done his best to be his normal self and, as far as he knew, none of his students had noticed how miserable he was inside. But at home, it had been impossible to keep up the façade and he supposed his depression and grief had been fairly obvious to his sons.

He had to make a change, he thought. He couldn't keep living in this kind of misery. With his mind totally consumed by the woman he loved.

The woman he loved. Yes, he could finally admit that he loved Stacy. That was a start, at least. But what was he going to do about it? Where was he going to find the courage to face her and what his feelings meant to the both of them?

Later that night, Win was sitting in a rocker in front of the fireplace when Joshua and Oliver surprised him with a mugful of coffee and a small plate of sugar cookies.

"Thanks, boys. This is really nice." He took a sip of the coffee and discovered the brew was really strong but sweetened just right. "So what have I done to deserve this special treatment? Or should I ask what have you done?"

Oliver was the first to speak. "We're not trying to make up for doing something bad, Dad. We just thought you looked tired tonight."

He eyed both boys as he picked up a cookie. Were they actually worried about him? The thought struck him hard.

"I am a little tired. But I'm okay."

They continued to stand a few steps away from his chair, watching him as though they expected him to collapse, or yell. Win couldn't decide which.

"Don't you boys have homework to do? I know you do, Joshua. I gave your class two chapters to read for a test Friday."

Joshua nodded. "I'll have the chapters read, Dad. And Oliver will get his homework done, too. We, uh…we just wanted to talk to you."

He sipped more of the hot coffee. Between it and the heat from the flames in the fireplace, he was beginning to warm up from the hour he'd spent wrapping several water pipes with insulation. The weather had rapidly taken a turn toward winter and he'd needed to get everything prepared.

"Okay. Are you guys wanting to ask me for something? Like a new horse? Or saddles?"

"No! We don't want nothing," Oliver declared.

"Don't use double negatives, Oliver! Do you want to sound dumb?" Joshua scolded. Then, just as quickly, his expression softened and he patted his little brother on the shoulder. "It's okay. I know you forget. I do, too, some-times."

Oliver gave his brother a grateful look, before he turned to his father. "We don't want to ask for stuff, Dad. We want to know why you don't smile anymore."

"Yeah. And why you don't see Ms. Abernathy anymore," Joshua added. "Don't you still like her?"

"We like her a lot," Oliver stated and then looked up to his brother. "Don't we, Joshua?"

Win was shocked at his sons' question and even more surprised to see his oldest son nod in agreement.

"We like Ms. Abernathy, Dad," Joshua said. "And we thought that—uh, you were going to start really liking her. And maybe make her our new mom."

Stunned, Win deliberately set the coffee and cookies aside then studied the boys' earnest faces. Since they'd moved to Bronco, he'd never seen either of them look so concerned or serious about anything.

"Joshua, do you really mean what you're saying?"

The teenager moved closer to Win's chair. "Sure, Dad. Don't you believe me?"

"I'd like to think you wouldn't say something so important without really meaning it. But it hasn't been that long ago that you were making a point of trying to steer me away from her and all women."

Joshua scuffed the toe of his boot against the rock hearth of the fireplace. "Yeah, but that was before I met Katrina. She's made me see that not all women are bad. Like Monica back in Whitehorn. I believed she really cared about me, but she turned out to be a cheat. And Tara—she was downright mean. Stacy would never be like her. I understand that now."

"I'm glad you've figured these things out, Joshua. But if you have the idea that Stacy would be like your mother, you're mistaken. Stacy is nothing like her."

Win watched in wonder as Joshua and Oliver both sat on the floor at his feet.

"Oliver doesn't remember Mom," Joshua said, "so he can't compare. But I remember, and I can see that Ms. Abernathy isn't like Mom. But I don't care about that and neither does Oliver. Ms. Abernathy is really nice, and I think Mom would like her. I think she'd be happy if Ms. Abernathy became a part of our family."

Hearing Joshua's words and seeing the eager expressions on his sons' faces was suddenly wiping away the fog in front of Win's eyes. If his teenaged son was strong enough to put the tragedy of losing his mother behind him, then Win could surely find the courage and strength to move his life forward.

Reaching out, he rubbed the top of Joshua's head and then Oliver's. "You're right, boys, your mother would like Stacy. And I think she'd be happy to know her sons had another mother to love them."

Oliver's face lit up like a Christmas tree. "Does that mean you're going to see Ms. Abernathy and be happy?"

Win took a deep breath and let it out. "It means I'm going to call Stacy tomorrow."

"Tomorrow?" Groaning, Joshua rolled his eyes. "Why not call her tonight?"

"Yeah, Dad, why not tonight?" Oliver seconded his brother's suggestion.

"Because it's far too late. She's probably getting ready for bed. And I need to think about what I'm going to say to her. I'm certain she's upset with me."

She was probably more than upset, Win thought. By now, she might even be hating him. The idea hurt, but he realized the pain he'd been going through had all been self-inflicted. And knowing that made it all that much harder to bear.

"Okay, why don't you let me and Oliver call her on the

way to school in the morning?" Joshua offered. "We'll invite her over here to the J Barb for dinner tomorrow night. She'll like that, Dad!"

"Yeah!" Oliver jumped to his feet and clapped his hands. "Me and Joshua can cook something good! That'll make her happy."

Joshua and Oliver had tried to make a few of their favorite dishes several times and Win had instructed them as much as possible with his limited knowledge of cooking, but preparing something edible for a guest would be a stretch for his sons.

"You boys believe you can cook something Stacy would like?"

Oliver straightened his shoulders as Joshua chucked his chin to a proud angle and said, "Dad, you know we make good spaghetti. It's easy."

"And we can have applesauce or pudding cups for dessert," Oliver added. "Ms. Abernathy will like those things, 'cause we have them at school for lunch."

Win was amazed by the excitement the boys were displaying. Not just over making a meal for Stacy, but also for planning to get her back on friendly terms with their father.

Wiping a hand over his eyes, he said, "Okay, you two, you have my permission to call Stacy and invite her to dinner. But I wouldn't get my hopes up that she'll agree to come. The last time I saw her, she wasn't very happy with me."

Stepping closer, Oliver lovingly patted his father's shoulder. "Don't worry, Dad. We'll talk her into it."

"Yeah, Dad. You just leave everything to me and Oliver," Joshua said then added, "Maybe you ought to get her some pretty flowers."

"Or buy her some fancy chocolate candy," Oliver was quick to suggest.

Flowers and candy? Win would do it. But he figured it would take more than those things to make Stacy forgive him.

Chapter Twelve

The next evening Stacy informed her parents she was driving over to the J Barb for dinner with Win and his sons. Her father merely arched one brow at her while her mother's mouth formed a perfect *O*. Thankfully, neither parent had caught her before she'd left the house to give her a lecture about thinking with her head instead of her heart.

Yet now, as Stacy drove onto J Barb land, she wondered if she was asking to be hurt and rejected all over again. When Joshua and Oliver had phoned her early this morning, she'd been more than surprised. Oliver had been first to speak and he'd been full of his usual bubbly enthusiasm when he'd insisted he and Joshua needed her to come try out their spaghetti recipe. He'd even added that they had a new shaker of parmesan cheese for further persuasion. As charming as Oliver had sounded, she'd hesitated to give the boy an answer and then Joshua had quickly taken over the phone. The teenager had insisted they wanted to fix her dinner to pay her back for the great picnic food she'd fed them at the park. Which had sounded logical enough to Stacy, but she'd still had to ask the obvious, "Has your Dad agreed to you boys having me over for dinner?"

"Oh sure, Ms. Abernathy. He's fine with it," Joshua had insisted and then Oliver had snatched up the phone and added, "Dad says its okay to have you over as long as we don't give you burned food."

After that Stacy had to accept the boys invitation, but she couldn't lie to herself. She'd been disappointed that Win hadn't called himself. But the fact that Joshua and Oliver had cared enough to invite her to dinner had filled her with a spark of hope that Win might possibly want to see her, too.

He probably wants this meeting so he can end things between you neatly and permanently, Stacy. He doesn't want to get into an ugly situation like the one he'd been in with Tara. That could be what this unexpected dinner invitation is all about.

The mocking voice in her head caused her foot to unwittingly slack off the accelerator. If that was Win's plan, she couldn't go through the humiliation. She'd rather go home and eat nails.

I happen to think Mr. Jackson is going to soon realize what a good thing he has in you.

Thankfully, Robin's remark suddenly pushed its way into doubts swirling around in her mind and she finished the last quarter mile to Win's house determined to face him with firm resolution.

The J Barb ranch house was a two-story structure surrounded by several tall evergreens. The outside walls consisted of a mixture of rough cedar siding and native rock, while the roof was galvanized tin. A large chimney of the same rock towered above the roof on the north end and the curl of wood smoke spiraling upward was a warming sight. Especially when she was trembling from the chill.

Or was the thought of seeing Win again making her shake? Either way, she had to get a grip. She wanted him to see she wasn't just a meek little second-grade teacher who couldn't hold her own with a rugged cowboy.

Tightening the rust-brown muffler around her neck, she left the car and began walking to a long porch with a roof supported by fat cedar post. Along the way, she was met by two friendly border collies and she paused long enough to greet them. The dogs yipped with excitement and followed her into the yard. As she and the pups headed for the porch, she noticed someone had thrown out wild birdseed beneath a tall cedar tree. Several red cardinals, along with a few sparrows, were pecking at the feed.

She was thinking how lovely the place looked when she heard a door open and close. The sound called her attention away from the birds and she went stock-still as she saw Win striding quickly toward her. He was holding one hand behind his back and she wondered if he'd injured his arm and made it immobile. However, as soon as he reached her, he pulled out a bouquet of white mums and red holly berries wrapped in green cellophane.

"Welcome to the J Barb, Stacy." He extended the bouquet toward her. "I hope you like chrysanthemums."

For a moment, she was so stunned, her tongue felt glued to the roof of her mouth and she swallowed twice in an effort to find her voice.

"I love chrysanthemums. Especially white ones." She looked down at the flowers nestled in the crook of her arm. "How did you know?"

"We're kindred spirits. Remember?"

Emotions pooled behind her breasts and rushed up to her throat. "I remember," she murmured then lifted her gaze to his face. "I don't understand, Win. Why—"

Before she could go on, his arm slipped around the back of her waist. "Let's go inside to talk. Where it's warm."

Her heart thumping with angst and hope, she said, "All right."

He guided her up the steps and across the porch. While he opened the door, Stacy glanced over her shoulder to see the dogs trotting toward the barn, which confirmed her assumption that the pair were working cattle dogs.

Inside the house, they walked from a short foyer and turned right into a large living room. She'd thought he would stop and seat her on the leather couch or one of the armchairs, but instead he guided her on to a door at the far end of the room.

Once they entered the small room, she realized the private space was an office, no doubt where he tended to schoolwork and the bookkeeping that went along with the ranch. There was a large desk equipped with a computer, and shelves built into one wall. The shelves were filled with books and other items that appeared to be souvenirs or mementos of special occasions. Along another wall was a couch covered in green tweed fabric.

Win led her over to the couch and waited for her to remove her coat. After she'd handed it to him, she took a seat on an end cushion. While she smoothed a hand over her blue-and-green-plaid skirt, he took his hat off and placed it and her coat on the corner of the desk.

With his head uncovered, her gaze went straight to his dark blond hair and suddenly she was remembering how the waves felt slipping through her fingers and how his skin had tasted as she'd pressed kisses over his face.

Clearing her throat, she looked past the desk to where a wide window looked out at a meadow dotted with evergreens and a herd of Black Baldy cattle gathered around a hay ring. She was still gazing at the peaceful scene when he walked over to where she sat.

"Here, let me put your flowers on the desk. We'll find a vase for them in a few minutes."

"Thank you."

She relinquished the bouquet to him and, after he'd placed it on the desk, he joined her on the couch.

When he reached for her hands, she very nearly pulled back from him, but quickly decided that avoiding his touch wouldn't accomplish anything. Especially when everything inside her was screaming to reach for him, to have him hold her tight in his arms.

"Win, what's going on? Where are the boys?" she asked.

"In the kitchen. Finishing making our dinner. I've told them I'd be bringing you in here to talk privately before we join them. So, they won't be barging through the door, if that's worrying you."

The soft laugh that erupted from her sounded like she was on the verge of hysteria. "Win, that's the least of my worries! I want to know why you let them invite me here to your ranch. After a week of hearing nothing from you, it's pretty darn obvious you've already quit on me and whatever we had between us. I honestly don't know why you bothered with flowers. I could've gotten the message without them."

His frown was almost comical. "Really? The boys seemed to think they'd send just the right message. And, by the way, you have a box of dark chocolates waiting for you in the kitchen. I think they want to give those to you personally."

"Flowers. Candy," she repeated dazedly. "I didn't realize Joshua and Oliver cared that much about me. Or that—"

Groaning helplessly, he gently pulled on her hands until her face was close to his. "The boys love you and so do I. That's why you're here. I can't say it any plainer than that."

She stared at him in stunned fascination. "You...love me? You're telling me that *now*? After the way you walked out on me in the cabin? I'm not a complete fool, Win. I don't believe everything a man tells me!"

His expression full of anguish, he shook his head. "Good thing you don't. Because I've said some things to you that weren't right. Like how I didn't want a woman in my life. That was the coward in me talking, Stacy. And it was the coward in me that left you in the cabin. I thought… I imagined you'd already figured out that I was running away from you."

"Why?" The question came out in a hoarse whisper. "I love you, Win. You don't need to run away from me. I'm not going to try to back you into a corner, or expect you to make some sort of lifelong commitment to me right now. I understood then and I still understand that you need time."

His hands were suddenly on her shoulders, holding them tightly as he gazed into her eyes. "You love me? Honestly?"

The sound that came out of her was something between a laugh and a sob. "Oh, Win. I think I've been in love with you from the first moment you said hello to me. That night after we met, I went home and told myself there wasn't such a thing as love at first sight. I told myself I was being stupid. But all that talking to myself didn't work."

"Thank God, it didn't work," he said fervently. Then, drawing her into his arms, he cradled her head against his shoulder. "Oh, sweetheart, that night after we made love at the cabin, I was rattled to the very core of my being. You were so beautiful and giving and wonderful. And when it struck me suddenly and deeply how very much I loved you, it terrified me. All I could think was the unbearable pain I'd go through if I ever lost you. And, to be honest, I was feeling guilty, too."

She pulled her head back far enough to look at him. "Guilty? Because you loved me?"

He nodded then groaned. "Yes, in a way. Because loving you made me realize I was finally leaving my marriage to Yvette. That was rough. I mean she'd been a part of my life for so long. She'd borne me two sons. And even after she died, she was still a part of my life—until now. Until you. It's taken me this long miserable week to finally come to terms with letting go and reaching for what I want in my life—and that is you and our children."

Her brows arched with surprise even as her heart was jumping with joy. "*Our* children?"

His forefingers tenderly touched her cheek. "Yes. *Our* children. You might be interested to know that Joshua and Oliver helped me see that Yvette would want them to have another mother. And they want you to be their new mom."

Stacy was so overcome with emotion that tears began to roll down her cheeks. "This is all so incredible, Win. These past days without any word from you have been worse than wretched. But I didn't want to give up on you. I wanted to believe that somehow you cared for me."

"Cared for you? Oh, darling, I want you to be my wife. And soon."

She realized she could finally smile, and it felt wonderful. "Soon?" she asked impishly. "You mean you don't want a long engagement?"

"No way! I want you right here in this house as my wife. As the mother of my sons, plus any brothers and sisters we'll give Joshua and Oliver. How does that sound?"

Laughing, now she asked, "Did you mean to say brother and sister in plural form?"

He chuckled. "I did. We need to keep the student population up so we can both have our teaching jobs," he joked and then his expression turned serious as his face drew close enough to kiss her cheek. "All kidding aside, I'd love to have two or three more kids. But only if you'd be happy to give them to me."

Her head was literally whirling with joy. "Oh, Win, I'd be more than happy. I can't wait for our life together to get started."

"Neither can I," he said.

With his hand at the back of her head, he pulled her mouth to his and, for long, glorious moments, he kissed her in a way that told Stacy he loved her and would always love her.

When he finally raised his head, he rubbed his cheek against hers. "Ready to go try the boys' spaghetti?" he asked.

"I am. But before we go out to the kitchen, there's one thing I'd like to say." Wrapping her arms around his neck, she rested her cheek against his shoulder. "I'm thrilled that I'm going to become the boys' mother, but I—well, I hope that Yvette would approve of me. That I can be as good a mother to Joshua and Oliver as she was."

He eased her head off his shoulder and, cupping his hands around the sides of her face, he smiled at her. "I think you should know that Joshua believes Yvette would be happy to know you're going to be his and Oliver's mother."

Joy flooded through her. "Oh Win, I'm so happy he feels that way. I want the boys to love me just as much as I need and want you to love me."

His arms tightened around her. "This past week, I kept imagining how I would feel if something took your life and took you away from me. But I've decided, Stacy, that I can't go around living my life in fear. I have to have trust and faith that we'll be together for a long, long time."

"Oh yes, my darling. After all, we're kindred spirits." She plastered kisses on his cheeks and chin and, finally, on his lips. "And kindred spirits stay together no matter what."

Laughing, he pulled her to her feet and fetched the bouquet of mums from the desk. "Come on. Let's go give the boys our good news."

When Stacy and Win entered the kitchen, the boys were sitting at a breakfast bar with their chins in their hands and looking worse than bored.

"Aren't you guys supposed to be cooking dinner?" Win asked.

As he and Stacy strolled to the middle of the room, Joshua and Oliver jumped off their barstools and stood anxiously eyeing them.

"The food is already done and the table in the dining room is set and ready. We're just waiting for you," Joshua said.

"Yeah. Just waiting to see if you two are happy now," Oliver said. "Are you?"

Win leveled a tender look at Stacy. "Are you happy?"

"Deliriously happy," she answered. "What about you?"

He chuckled. "I think my boots have sprouted wings. I'm pretty sure I flew here to the kitchen."

Loving the joy she saw on his face, she chuckled with him. "Maybe you did."

"Oh, Dad, you sound silly," Oliver said.

"Sometimes a person acts silly when he's really, really happy." He handed the bouquet of flowers to Joshua. "Put these in a vase of water for Stacy. Then you two join us in the living room. We want to talk to you before we eat."

Out in the living room, Stacy and Win sat on a couch that faced the fireplace while Joshua and Oliver sat on a braided rug at their feet.

"Is this going to be a long lecture?" Oliver asked. "'Cause we're really hungry."

Stacy looked at Win and burst out laughing. "We'd better make this fast."

"Right." Grinning from ear to ear, Win turned to his sons. "Stacy is going to become a part of our family. She's agreed to become my wife and your mother. How do you guys feel about that?"

A look of pure joy swept over Oliver's face while Joshua held his reaction to a little grin.

"Oooh, this is great. Really, really great!" Oliver practically shouted.

Joshua was doing his best to hold on to his fifteen-year-old coolness, but Stacy could see his eyes were twinkling with happiness.

"Yeah, Dad," Joshua said. "This is awesome. It's just what I—uh, that's just what me and Oliver want. To have Stacy make us a whole family again."

Stacy's heart was suddenly overflowing with love for Win and the two boys, who were soon going to be her sons, too.

"'A whole family,'" Stacy repeated. "Thank you, Joshua. You couldn't have said anything nicer. And you, too, Oliver. You guys are both very special to me, and I know we're going to be happy together as a family."

Looking as pleased as punch, Oliver looked from Stacy to his father. "When are you getting married? Tomorrow?"

Joshua gently elbowed his brother in the ribs. "Silly. It takes time to have a wedding! Like a week or so!"

Oliver looked crestfallen. "Oh. That's a long time."

Stacy and Win exchanged amused looks before he said, "A wedding takes longer than either of you think. And we'll need to have a few days away from our teaching jobs when we have the ceremony. That means we'll have to wait until the first long school break."

"Like Christmas!" Oliver burst out with excitement. "We get a lot of days off from school then!"

Stacy felt just as excited as Oliver and she looked eagerly at Win. "I would love to have a Christmas wedding, Win. What about you?"

He gently squeezed her hands. "Since it can't be tomorrow, I can't think of a more joyous time for a wedding. But I'm thinking we'll need more time for a honeymoon. What do you say we save it for summer break?"

"And take the boys with us on a family honeymoon?" Stacy quickly suggested while casting a coy grin at Win. "Since I'm marrying into a family of cowboys, you all might like to go watch the big rodeo in Cheyenne. From what I understand there's also a huge midway and plenty of fun things going on at the same time. That is, if you'd like it, Win. And the boys agree."

His gaze made a tender search of her face. "I'll be with you and the boys. Nothing could make me happier."

Clapping his hands, Oliver jumped excitedly to his feet while Joshua's grin spread from ear to ear.

"We like it," Joshua said.

"A whole lot!" Oliver added.

A thought suddenly struck Win as his look encompassed Stacy and his sons. "Well, speaking of rodeos, we don't have to wait until this summer to go to one. In a few weeks, the Golden Buckle Rodeo will be happening here in Bronco."

"I've been hearing some of the teachers talk about it," Stacy told him. "They're all excited about seeing Brooks Langtree. He's supposed to be a big rodeo star. In fact, he's the first Black rodeo rider to ever be awarded the Golden Buckle."

Win nodded. "Anthony has been talking about Brooks,

too. He says it's been thirty years since Langtree's been to Bronco and he doesn't want to miss seeing him at the rodeo."

"Thirty years," Stacy said in amazement. "Then the man hasn't been here since I was born! Something important must be drawing him back here."

"Money, most likely," Win joked then said, "I'm only teasing. I'm guessing the man must have some sort of ties to Bronco."

Stacy shot him a knowing smile. "Like an old sweetheart?"

Win chuckled. "You would think in those terms."

"We don't want to forget the Bronco Harvest Festival, Dad." Joshua spoke up. "I've already promised Katrina I'll try to win her a teddy bear on the midway."

Oliver could hardly contain his joy as he hopped on one boot and then the other. "You know what's going to be the most fun? We're going to have a real mom to go with us."

Stacy wasn't going to spoil Oliver's happiness by pointing out she and Win would have to be married before she'd legally be his and Joshua's real mom. In her heart, she was already the boys' mother.

"A real mom is exactly right, son." Win stood and helped Stacy to her feet. "Now that we have everything settled, I think it's time we had dinner. And I have a surprise for you guys. We don't have to eat applesauce for dessert. I bought brownies from the deli and hid them in the pantry."

"Wow! Brownies! I'm gonna go find them and put them on the table!" Oliver shouted and took off in a run toward the kitchen.

"You better not drop them, Oliver!" Joshua called out as he trotted after his little brother.

As Win and Stacy followed the boys at a slower pace, he looked over at her. "We had brownies at the picnic, remember? I thought it might fit the occasion this evening—especially if you agreed to marry me. The only difference is, these brownies aren't homemade."

Slipping her arm through his, she smiled up at him. "Who cares if they're store bought or homemade? It's the thought that counts."

Pausing, he drew her into his arms and, as he kissed her, she knew for certain that Win had learned his lesson about love and trust and believing in always. And she'd learned that following her heart might've been a risky venture, but in the end, it had led her straight to the family she'd always wanted.

* * * * *

Look for the next installment in the new continuity
Montana Mavericks: The Trail to Tenacity
That Maverick of Mine
by Kathy Douglass
On sale October 2024
Wherever Harlequin books
and ebooks are sold.

And don't miss the first book
Redeeming the Maverick
by New York Times bestselling
author Christine Rimmer

Available now!